CHOSEN BY THE PRINCE

CALYOPE ADAMS

Contents

For the readers

FOREWORD

This is an expanded third edition of *Chosen By The Prince*

CHOSEN BY THE PRINCE

He can choose only one woman. He chose her...

Spoiled socialite Jillian is at the Royal Palace for a party when the King's Advisor pulls her aside. He informs her that she's been selected to be the Prince's personal plaything for the remainder of her days, or until he releases her from servitude. It is her duty as a loyal subject to try and please him, no matter what the cost to her pride.

Jillian stares at the handsome Prince in shock as the guards lock the jewel encrusted collar around her neck. He doesn't even like her!

He's been giving her odd, dark looks for years. What she doesn't realize is that he's been biding his time, waiting for her to grow up, to be ready to be *Chosen By The Prince...*

PROLOGUE

There she was.

The Prince stared hungrily at the young beauty from the relative privacy of the royal carriage. No one had spotted him yet. He planned to keep it that way.

He'd come to the park today just hoping to see her. He knew she would bow and curtsy like the rest of her friends if he made an appearance. And yet, there would be a flash of fire in her eyes.

Not of lust.

Of definiace.

A defiance that made him long for the day he would claim her. He would tame her to his hand, making her serve him as only she could. Only she could quench the desire that burned low and deep in his belly.

He let his eyes trail over the lithe curves of her body. She was ready. He'd waited long enough for her to mature.

Tomorrow. She would be his tomorrow.

Lady Jillian had no idea of what was to come. He smiled, watching her lord it over her friends. The other girls followed her, like baby chicks and a mother hen.

But none came close to her, try as they might. No woman in the realm could match Lady Jillain.

Her beauty. Her intelligence. Or her pride.

She was such a feisty little thing. He knew she would test his patience.

But he also knew that he would win.

PART ONE - JILLIAN

Jillian stood with her friends, laughing and gossiping. They sipped a sweet infusion of rose petals in liquor, savoring the flavor. The food at the Palace was always the best, and the celebration today was no exception. The cause for the celebration was somewhat mysterious however.

Jillian was noticeable from afar, her looks making her stand out from the other girls. There was an innocence about her, as well as a sensuality, in the dark gold of her eyes and gleam of her bronze colored hair. Her lips pouted playfully as her friends whispered about the Prince. He was just over there, standing in the center of several young men. He was staring at her, she realized with a start.

Prince Maximilian always had an odd look on his face when he looked at her. He looked determined... and hungry somehow.

A shiver ran down her back. So what if the Prince didn't like her? What difference did it make? Her father was about to announce her engagement to the second most eligible man in all the land, the young Duke Henry. She smiled to herself. Her friends would be green with envy when they knew. It wasn't her fault that her dowry was the largest, or that her face held the classical lines of beauty that made all men give her a second glance, and a third, and a fourth...

Her face was oval, with her huge gold eyes dominating her delicate features and tawny skin. High cheekbones, a small nose and a rosebud of a mouth that invited a man to kiss it. None had yet of course but she was sure that... well, she wasn't exactly sure what would happen then. Like other well bred virgins, she had been deliberately kept in the dark about what happens between a man and a woman behind closed doors. She was sure it was exciting though. And she'd find out soon enough!

A soft blush tinged her cheeks as she caught the Prince staring at her again. He was standing with the Duke, their heads tilted slightly together as they watched her. The Duke was fair while the Prince had dark hair and piercing green eyes. He was incredibly handsome and well built, tall and slim with an aristocratic bearing. But for some reason, Jillian always found herself irritated by his smug good looks. Now was no exception.

She smiled pointedly at Duke Henry then tossed her head at the Prince, glaring at him archly over her shoulder and turning her back. She caught a glimpse of the slow smile that was sliding across his face... before her friends caught her attention again, urging her to taste the strawberry tarts.

The luncheon party was drawing to a close as Jillian followed her friends to the gate to await their carriages. She was tired and a bit tipsy from the beverages pushed on her all day. She stifled a yawn as the King's advisor swept into the room followed by a contingent of guards. They marched forward with purpose. It almost looked as if they were coming straight toward her...

Jillian already had her cloak on and was standing with her friends as they stared at Valspar, open mouthed.

"Lady Jillian, please come with me."

Her eyes widened as he took her elbow firmly and guided her back into the main hall.

"What's this all about?"

"Your cloak, if you please."

He held his hands out, waiting until she removed her cloak and placed it in his hands. What choice did she have really? He passed it to a servant who was hovering nearby, who took it away.

Well, that was odd.

"Please sit."

He guided her to a seat in the corner of the great hall. There were still people enjoying the party on the other side of the room, where the Prince was leaning against the windows, smiling lazily.

She realized the Prince was watching her again. But not her face. He was looking at her body. She stiffened and sat down abruptly.

How rude!

She turned her attention to the older man who stood before her. The guards had fanned out around her chair, blocking her view of the exit. The whole thing was disconcerting.

"It is my great honor to inform you that you have been selected."

Her mouth opened a bit as she stared at him.

"Selected for what? I don't understand..."

He looked at her closely, a hard look on his face. An odd feeling was settling in Jillian's stomach. Dread... It was dread.

"The Prince has chosen you to be his Sofriquette."

"His... what?"

"Surely you know who Sephina is?"

Jillian nodded. Sephina was the stunningly beautiful older woman who accompanied the King everywhere. She was some sort of advisor, always standing or sitting off to the side, always within the King's periphery. She rarely spoke or was acknowledged by guests. The Queen ignored her completely.

"She is the King's Sofriquette."

Jillian stared at him blankly, missing the point.

"She serves the King."

"I see. Well, the Prince has plenty of servants and courtiers. I don't see why he needs another one."

He crossed his arms and stared at her as if she was slow witted.

"The Sofriquette has a unique position, one that she alone can fulfill."

"Again, I don't see what this has to do with me."

The advisor smiled and raised his finger. A servant brought over a heavy box and placed it on a table in front of her.

"The Prince is allowed to choose one woman. One, for his entire life. She will be his outlet, providing him with the comfort and ease that no one else can. He has chosen you for this honored position."

"Comfort and ease?"

"Do you know anything of what happens between a man and a woman?"

She shook her head, sneaking a look at the Prince across the room. He was still watching her, an intense look on his face. He looked... hungry again. Ravenous, really. Somebody should bring him something to eat. He was the Prince after all.

"Well, that is the service you are to provide for the Prince. It's of a private nature. You are to be available to him at all times. To refuse any request is considered treason."

Jillian inhaled sharply.

"There is no refusal of this position. To do so would mean you and your family would forfeit your lands and your lives."

Her eyes widened. Suddenly it felt difficult to breath.

"But I'm too be married soon!"

The King's advisor simply shook his head and lifted the top of the box. But Jillain wasn't finished yet.

"You expect me to give that up to become his- his-"

She started to stand but one of the guards was suddenly behind her, pressing her shoulders back into the chair.

"Be still."

She looked down. Inside the box was a wide banded necklace- no, it was a collar. It was made of heavy gold and studded with a fortune in jewels. In the front was a small hook from which dangled a gold chain.

She gasped, realizing that a similar collar was worn by Sephina, the King's Sofriquette... he was often seen holding the chain loosely in his hand. Did everyone but her understand what that meant? Had she really been so blind?

"This collar symbolizes your submission to your lord and master."

"Wait-"

She was shaking as he lifted the circlet up and came to stand behind her, lowering the collar around her throat. She swallowed as he slid the lock into place.

"Wait! I- can't I speak to him? Surely he hasn't made his mind up yet."

The lock twisted behind her, sealing with a loud thunk. She closed her eyes, feeling the weight of it holding her down. Valspar moved around the chair until he stood in front of her again.

"Actually the choice was made several years ago. He chose to wait until now to claim you."

"Until I was about to be married! He hates me! He's punishing me for-"

"I suggest you lower your voice. You are already the Sofriquette and will be expected to behave accordingly."

He softened his voice, leaning toward her, an earnest look in his eyes.

"This is an honorable task that you fulfill. A Prince must not be distracted by unfulfilled lusts or allowed to sow bastards everywhere. You will allow him to be focused on his duties, knowing that you are there to ease him whenever the need arises. You do not serve only him, you serve the nation."

"But he is to be married next year, to the Princess of Haight!"

"Yes, but he did not chose her. He must be allowed one choice, one thing he can have simply for himself, as a man. He chose you."

She lowered her head, tears streaming down her face. The collar was lined in something soft- a silk velvet-but it still felt uncomfortable against her throat.

"Punishing you for what?"

She looked up at him. He had a look of curiosity on his face.

"You said before he was punishing you..."

"Nothing. It was nothing."

But it wasn't. They had just been children, the Prince several years older, when she'd bested him in a game. He'd been right behind her, racing through the maze for the prize but her hands and closed on the golden apple first.

He's stared at her, breathing heavily and commanded that she give him the apple. She'd refused. He had smiled coldly at her then, sending shivers down her spine.

This was his answer to that long ago slight. She closed her eyes, knowing her pride and swift legs had brought this fate on her... and her family. She could do nothing to stop his revenge...

Dear god.

"I suggest you dry your tears now. It would be best if no one saw you crying. You will be escorted to your new chambers. Please let the servants know if there is anything you require."

"I require to go home!"

He smiled tightly.

"This is your home now. You best get used to the idea quickly."

The guards grabbed her arms and lifted her, surrounding her as they swept her from the hall. She looked sideways, seeing the Prince as he laughed with his guests. His eyes shifted to her as she passed him, burning into her. He looked triumphant.

Her chamber was spacious and in a special part of the castle she had never seen before. Her room was up a hidden spiral staircase, apparently immediately above the Prince's chamber. It was luxuriously decorated, with a huge bed and soft pillows in front of the fireplace. Everything was oversized and comfortable, even the window seat. She even had a sitting room with a desk that overlooked the gardens.

She looked around the room in a daze as servants bustled around her. They were running a bath in an adjoining chamber she hadn't seen yet. The door closed behind her and she felt a maid's hands removing her gown.

"What-"

"We must bathe you Sofiquette, and quickly. There is a banquet tonight and the you must be ready for him before then if at all possible. There is much to do to prepare you."

There was no need to tell her who 'he' was. She held still as they removed her gown and underthings. There were three maids in the room with her, guiding her into the enormous bathing chamber. There was a high padded table to the side as well as a low bench and a cabinet covered with oils and tools she didn't recognize. The tub was set low in the ground, more of a pool than a bathtub. It was carved out of an enormous slab of marble. She'd never seen anything like it.

Her mind was in turmoil as they pushed her toward the water, dunking her under the surface.

"Please stand."

She did as she was asked and they began washing her, soaping her body meticulously. They pressed her under the water again then led her to the bench where she was asked to lay down on her back. They applied a paste to her arms and legs and between her legs. She pulled away when they pressed their fingers to her cleft but they held her firm, one maid slapping the sole of her foot sharply with an iron rod.

"Ow!"

"Be still Sofriquette. You must let us complete our task or you will be punished, as will we."

She held still then, the sole of her foot smarting. The paste they had spread on her tingled on her skin, smelling like burnt sugar. They busied themselves with her hair as they waited for the paste to take effect, trimming her long locks and massaging oil into her scalp. Then they each took a sharp blade and slid it over her skin, removing the paste along with every bit of her body hair.

She held still, the sensation of being hairless disturbing her. They led her back to the bathing pool where she immersed herself again, the water running constantly, replenishing itself so that it was always warm and clean.

She stood as they rubbed a course cream over her skin, polishing it. They dunked her again and finally led her out of the tub to dry her with soft towels. She lay on the table again as they massaged sweet smelling oils into her skin.

Their hands felt so soft on her skin, relaxing her, until they touched her breasts. She slid to the side, trying to evade the personal touch. The sharp sting of the rod slapped her foot again, making her moan. When their hands glided to her cleft, oiling her thoroughly, she gritted her teeth, forcing herself to be still.

They led her to a stool where she sat as they skillfully applied makeup to her eyes and lips, darkening them. Her hair was curled and twisted back so it cascaded over her shoulders, leaving her profile exposed. They twined pearls through her hair, letting the strands dangle against her bare skin.

She stood when they were done and followed them into her chamber, nude. They dressed her then, starting with undergarments of the softest silk. There was a mirror where she could see herself. The white lace was sheer, clearly showing her nipples through the corset and the dark line of her sex, her pouty lips outlined clearly, now that she was completely bare.

She looked away, hardly believing it was her own body. She felt so removed from what was happening to her.

One of the maids knelt in front of her and slipped a finger along her slit, applying one last cream. She would never get used to these intimate touches...

"Oh! What is that?"

"Honey."

"What for?"

The maids looked at each other, not answering. They slid a gown over her head. It was lightweight silk, threaded with real gold. The color matched her eyes perfectly. The back dipped low, revealing her back nearly to the top of her round, high bottom. The dress showed the hard points of her nipples clearly.

She frowned. She looked obscene. Why were her breasts doing that?

"It's the cream."

"What?"

"We applied a stimulant to your skin, Sofriquette."

"*Oh.*"

That explained the tingling, centered on her nipples and also between her legs...

She felt completely out of her element. She knew nothing of what was expected of her. She wanted to go home... She pushed the thought aside as tears started to well up in her eyes. If she ruined her makeup they would surely punish her again. She forced herself to relax as they lowered the collar over her head, snapping it into place.

Her tears threatened again as she felt the cold weight of it against her throat. She stared at herself in the mirror. Her skin and hair and body were displayed in such a way that made her look sublime and tender, good enough to eat. At the same time she looked regal, like a queen and a slave at the same time.

Maybe that was the point.

The door opened behind her. The maids curtsied quickly, leaving her. She turned, knowing it was him. She lowered her eyes, afraid to look at him.

She heard the door shut and swallowed, her nerves returning full force. She forced herself to raise her eyes and face him. He inhaled sharply as their eyes met. He didn't look mean or angry as she feared. He looked... awestruck.

"My god..."

His voice sounded low and harsh to her ears. He was across the room, towering over her in an instant. She could see the rich cloth of his evening clothes as she stared straight in front of her. He was so tall...

His hands reached out and slid over her shoulders, gliding across her collarbone and over her breasts. He moaned softly as she turned her head to the side. The humiliation of her situation was making her face burn. He could do whatever he wanted to her, touch her however he liked and there was nothing she could do about it.

He grasped her chin lightly, raising her face so she looked at him. She could not hide the defiance in her eyes.

He smiled at her sensually.

"You are exquisite little one."

She looked away from him, annoyed by his possessive gaze, so sure of his ownership of her. He laughed softly.

"Such a little brat you are. We'll soon see to that. It's too bad the banquet is about to start..."

She tossed her head a bit, swallowing against the collar. He frowned.

"Is that too tight?"

She looked at him quickly, opening her mouth. She had no idea what to say to him...

"It's- a little."

He stared at her thoughtfully.

"We'll fix it. Unfortunately there's not enough time now, but you don't have to wear it later when we are alone."

She said nothing, staring stonily at the ground. He chuckled again and lifted something from his pocket. The chain. He fitted it to the hook in her collar and slid the handle over his hand. She stared at it, his large hand holding the leather circle firmly.

"Come. You will walk in front of me so I can look at you."

She stepped out of the room into the hallway. There were four guard there. Two of them led the way. She fell into step behind them, feeling the Prince's eyes on her bare back. The other two guards brought up the rear.

She stared straight ahead, her back straight, as they walked through the castle. Everyone was watching them, all eyes on her. She felt naked, her skin tingling under the light silk of the gown. She refused to react in any way. She had her pride after all. Too much of it most likely.

They walked through the hall to the dining chamber where the Royal table was set high on a dais. There was another level with a small table set off to the side before the main floor, where most of the nobles and dignitaries sat. She was guided to the small table where Sephina already stood, waiting. The King and Queen were already seated. The Prince joined them, still holding her leash. It stretched between them, making a clanging sound as it hit the floor.

She was given a seat that faced sideways, so the Prince could watch her easily. Sephina had her back to the main floor so she was also within the King's view. She smiled at Jillian softly. They waited as the Prince took his seat, and then they sat down.

"You look lovely."

The woman's voice was so soft she nearly didn't hear it. She glanced at her sideways as they were served wine. Sephina looked utterly serene, her eyes demurely lowered.

"And terrified."

Jillian lifted her eyes to Sephina again, but the woman was staring down at her empty plate, a soft smile on her lips.

"Not that I blame you. When it was my turn, I had months of instruction before I was claimed. Times have changed."

Jillian sipped her wine, trying to ignore the Prince who was openly staring at her. He grinned, tugging on her chain. She flashed her eyes at him angrily.

"I would try to avoid aggravating him right now, my dear."

The servants moved around them, laying plates along the tables. All except theirs. Finally a small plate of salad was placed before each of them.

"Do they intend to starve us?"

Sephina's lips tilted up again.

"It's best to eat small meals throughout the day. I have my biggest meal in the morning."

"Why?"

Sephina's eyes lifted to hers conspiratorially.

"Because you don't want to be full at night. That's the time he's most likely to call upon you."

Oh. She wished she hadn't asked.

"Of course, if he doesn't require you for the evening you can always have food brought to your room."

Jillian took a dainty bite of her salad, trying to mimic the older woman.

"Though in your case, I suspect you will get little rest for a good long time."

Jillian almost choked on her wine. The older woman smiled at her, hiding a laugh.

"I wish I could give you advice my dear but I was specifically told not to. If and when the time comes to formally instruct you, I will be happy to do so."

Jillian stared down at her plate. She was having trouble breathing suddenly. She could feel the people from one side looking her over, inspecting her. On the other side, the Prince's hot gaze seemed to burn into her skin.

She felt tingly all over and the light coating of honey between her legs was sticky... She glanced at the Prince. He was smiling as if he'd just been given a great prize. She was sure he knew about everything they had done to her. Everyone in the room most likely did. She wanted to crawl under the table and hide.

"You know nothing of what is to come?"

Jillian shook her head 'no', a little more violently than she meant to. The pearls clinked against the collar. She looked up, her eyes wide with mounting panic. The Prince was frowning at her. Sephina looked alarmed.

"Hush now, it will all be alright, I promise you. Drink your wine."

She let out a breathy laugh, feeling slightly hysterical. She sipped the wine, distracted by the bitter taste as she got closer to the bottom of the glass.

"What is that?"

"It's an aphrodisiac."

Jillian stared at the woman. The whole world had gone mad.

"It's a drug?"

"It's harmless. And you are expected to drink and eat everything they put in front of you so try and hide your reactions."

"I hate this. I hate all these rules."

She was whispering, a calm look pinned to her face. Sephina nodded approvingly.

"That's it, you are learning. Trust me, many of the rules are for your own protection."

"From what?"

"If there was not a rule about seating us separately, you would find yourself laying on that table being eaten instead of the meal."

Jillian shot her a horrified glance.

"Not literally. Oh, I'm not helping at all, am I? It's just hard not to notice how he's looking at you."

Jillian slid her eyes to the Prince again. He was brooding, his eyes hard on her face. His father said something to him and he turned away momentarily.

"That's how he always looks at me. He hates me. He's just doing this to humiliate me."

Sephina raised her eyebrows at that.

"Is that what you think? I would say he hates waiting for something he wants rather badly. He's been waiting for some time from what I understand."

Jillian lifted her chin.

"Yes, he's been waiting to shame me."

"Hmmm... I wouldn't be too sure."

They ate the rest of their salads in silence, each being served another glass of wine, this one more bitter than the last. The whole room was gorging themselves on meats and pies but they just sat there with nothing in front of them. Finally they were each served a small plate of berries. Jillian watched as Sephina picked up a berry and delicately slid it between her lips.

"Use your fingers."

She did her best to imitate the other woman, certain this was part of some ritual she had to follow. She was trying to do her best, knowing how vital her compliance was. She slipped a berry between her lips and bit down, the tart flavor exploding in her mouth.

She ate each berry as Sephina did, one at a time. She looked up and the Prince was staring at her mouth, transfixed. She stopped abruptly. Sephina shook her head lightly.

"Finish them. The meal is almost over."

Jillian ate the last few berries resentfully, turning to the side so she didn't have to see the Prince watching her. It made her feel very strange, warm and jumpy at the same time.

Finally things seemed to be wrapping up. The Prince stood abruptly and two guard were quickly at her side.

"Good luck, my dear. You'll be fine."

Jillian gave the woman a last searching look then stood up, staring straight ahead. She ignored the knowing glances being cast her way. She followed the guards back the way they came, taking the main staircase this time. They were going somewhere else. Maybe he'd changed his mind- maybe-

A door opened onto a huge bedroom. His room. She knew it instantly. The room was extravagantly luxurious and so masculine. A fire was burning in the enormous hearth, pillows strewn before it. There were two bottles of wine on the table with two glasses.

The door shut behind her, making her jump. She turned and there he was, staring at her with an odd look on his face. He looked very... focused.

His eyes slid down over her body and back to her face. He walked toward her purposefully, making her take a step back. He narrowed his eyes, reaching for her. She closed her eyes tightly, forcing herself to be still.

"Are you truly so frightened of me?"

She opened her eyes. He was inches away, his chest giving off waves of heat. He lifted his hands to her shoulders. She just looked at him, utterly panicked. He sighed and reached around her throat. He was going to strangle her!

The lock holding her collar in place snapped open. She lifted her hand to her throat, rubbing it. He watched her, his mouth open. His eyes drifted to her lips. She knew suddenly without a doubt that he was going to kiss her.

Her first kiss.

He lowered his dark head and pressed his lips into hers. His lips were warm and softer than she'd thought a man's lips would be... he slanted his mouth over hers insistently, sliding his tongue between her lips. She gasped and tried to pull back.

The Prince groaned and lifted his head.

"Don't."

She closed her eyes as he kissed her again. Warmth was spiraling through her body as his tongue pushed into her mouth, tangling with her own, stroking her firmly.

Oh god... she felt like her body was on fire.

He pulled her against him, her chest slamming into his, her breasts smashing up against his shirt. He moaned again and the kiss deepened. She felt his body on her, and something pressing against her stomach. Something big and hard.

She twisted away from him, before she realized what she was doing. He was panting, staring at her, anger and need darkening his face. Her hand flew to her mouth.

Oh god, what had she done?

He strode away from her, his hand reaching for the door.

"Wait-"

He stopped.

"Please-"

Had she just signed her family's death warrants? She had to try and stop him- she had to-

He turned and looked at her, waiting.

"I was just surprised. I didn't- I don't know what I'm supposed to do."

His eyes searched her face, wanting to believe her. He sighed and closed his eyes. His hand dropped from the doorknob. She swallowed convulsively, feeling like she might faint. He was watching her again.

"It's not your fault."

Her eyes flew to his face.

"I know this is all very strange for you. Can you try to- trust me?"

She stared at him, then at the ground, nodding jerkily. He walked back over to her and held out his hand. She put her hand inside his. It was so warm, so much bigger than hers.

She took a deep breath and lifted her eyes to his. He smiled at her warmly. Perhaps Sephina was right... perhaps he didn't hate her after all...

"Come."

He led her to the pillows in front of the fire. There was a white satin blanket covering the plush wool rug. She lowered herself down beside him, letting him pull her back into his arms. They stared into the fire together. He was giving her time she realized. A strange feeling was rising in her throat. He was trying to be kind.

"Do you have any idea how long I've waited for you?"

She shook her head softly, his warm breath tickling her ear.

His shifted his body closer to hers, pulling her against his chest. His hands wandered up and down her body, just shy of her breasts. She moaned softly, surprised by how good it felt.

"Too long."

His low voice sent a thrill through her body. She wanted his hands to stop moving, to close over her breasts. Oh.... she was so confused as her body and her mind seemed to battle.

"Hmmmm..."

He murmured against her neck as his hands finally closed over her breasts. Her nipples soaked up the warmth, poking the palms of his hands. Oh god, it felt so good. She never wanted it to stop...

He was rocking his groin against her hips slowly as he kneaded her breasts, his lips nibbling at her throat. Waves of sensation washed through her and she pushed back against him, feeling his hardness against her round bottom. He groaned as she arched into him.

"Oh god... oh yes..."

He lifted her slightly, laying her back on the pillows and pressing his body down on top of hers. He kissed her again, but this time she kissed him back. He'd shown her mercy and now he was showing her desire... she felt her fear receding, replaced by something else... something *urgent*.

His hands were at her breasts again, parting her dress down the center. She hadn't realized it would give way so easily. Her body was bare now, only covered by the sheer lace of her underthings...

He moaned in ecstasy as he stared down at her glowing flesh, lowering his mouth to her belly, kissing her, moving up to her breasts. He slid a finger under the lace and her breasts sprang free, the corset obviously designed to come apart at the slightest touch.

Ohhh...

He was worshipping her breasts now, holding them and kissing them passionately, sucking her nipples into his warm mouth. She realized that her hands were in his hair, tangling in the soft waves as she held him in place, urging him to taste her, wanting more.

"Oh!"

She gasped as he tugged her nipple sharply, chuckling. Then he was kissing her belly again, his hands sliding her panties off over her hips, bearing her mound to him, her pink lips shining softly in the firelight.

He moaned and he lowered his mouth to her, his tongue teasing the slit where her pouting lips met.

She squealed and tried to get away, shocked by what he was doing. He used his weight to hold her hips down. His hands grabbed her wrists as she instinctively tried to push him away. He stared up at her, seeing the panic in her eyes, unmoved this time.

"Don't deny me, Jillian."

She stared into his hard eyes, seeing the futility in her actions. She was breathing heavily as he waited to see what she would do. She closed her eyes tightly and pulled her hands away, giving him access to her most intimate place. He lowered his head instantly, letting his tongue slide up her tiny slit again. He moaned into her, his breath fanning her bare lips.

"Hmmmm... you taste so sweet."

He was licking her as if she was the most delicious thing he'd ever tasted. His tongue slid up and down her nether lips, flicking at the sensitive nub above. Her hips circled against him involuntarily, her shyness battling with the intense pleasure his mouth was giving her. He moaned again, sensing her surrender and let his tongue slip inside her, pressing between her plump petals and into her tight femininity.

"Ohhhh!"

She made her hands into fists to stop herself for pushing him away again. The sensation was too much. Dear god! His hand held her down as he plundered her with his mouth, his tongue stroking her intimately, deep inside. Her hips shot up into the air as a strange shuddering feeling come over her, wracking her body with shivers.

"Oh, oh, oh, OH!"

He held her hips in place against his mouth, his tongue working her insistently as she shook uncontrollably. It seemed to go on forever. Finally he let her body slide back to the floor, his eyes on her face as her head tossed helplessly.

"Oh god Jillian..."

He shifted his weight over her, opening his clothes. She felt his hot skin against her chest, her nipples pressing against his bare chest. He was doing something with his hands, removing his pants and quickly guiding his manhood to her tight slit. She was slick with her juices as he pressed forward, sliding the tip inside her. The skin on his shaft was so hot... His cock stretching her open wide. He pressed forward experimentally, coming into contact with her barrier.

"Jillian, oh god... do you know what happens now?"

She opened her eyes to stare up at him. The Prince stared down at her, an intense longing in his slanted green eyes. She shook her head, mindless. She wanted him to move- to press into her- oh!

Her hips moved against him instinctively. He shut his eyes, his hips jerking.

"Oh- hmmmmfffff- Jillian I have to hurt you now. But it's only this once, I promise."

She barely heard him, her hips rocking against him, making tiny circles... in the back of her mind she wondered what she had been so afraid of after all.

"Oh god... you're so tight Jillian. Unfff... I'm sorry but I can't wait-"

He shifted back and drove forward, tearing through her sheath. She tensed up as the pain washed through her, sweeping away the desire. He held her tightly as she thrashed in his arms, wanting to get away, to move away from the huge shape inside her, causing her pain.

"Don't move! Oh god-"

He pushed inside her again, making her cry out. She looked up to see his face squeezed tightly in agony as he fought his instincts with every fiber of his being.

"Okay... hmmmfff... unnnfff... just... don't move."

He opened his eyes and looked down at her. She was watching him, looking like a cornered animal. He tried to soothe her with a smile that looked more like a grimace, his huge cock pinning her to the bed.

"Oh god! Hmmfff... I can't-"

He lowered his hand to her face, cupping her cheek.

"I'm sorry Jillian. I can't wait any longer."

He pulled out of her slightly, driving back in almost immediately. Then again. The pain was receding now, but it still felt uncomfortable. He rocked his manhood into her again and again, his face a mask of ecstasy.

"Oh god... oh god..."

He grunted with pleasure with each stroke, pounding his hips into hers as he slid in and out of her tight slit. She gasped as her body started to respond again, her nipples scratched by his chest as he slid against her.

"Oh..."

Her soft moan catapulted him out of control, his hips pumping his shaft into her wildly. She was writhing against him now, so close to reaching her peak, but he froze before she could get there, his body convulsing as he filled her with his seed.

He lay on top of her, his breathing ragged as he struggled to regain control of his body. She was quivering, overstimulated where he held her open with his thick root. He stared down at her as he slid out, leaning down to kiss her briefly. Then he stood and walked into an open doorway across the room. The bathroom.

She lay there, afraid to move. Her body felt shattered into a thousand pieces. He was back quickly, his body lit softly by the fire light.

He was beautiful, she thought as she gazed up at him. His body was hard and strong and perfectly proportioned. His shoulders broad, his chest chiseled and his hips- oh. His shaft was rising again as he watched her eyes move over his body. Her startled gaze flew to his face as he smiled at her.

He knelt and pressed a warm washcloth to her cleft, making her wince. He swallowed, closing his eyes, just holding the cloth against her. It was very soothing.

He put it aside and gathered her up in his arms again. He kissed her tenderly, pulling back as she pressed against the full length of his body. He laughed ruefully.

"Oh god, don't touch me like that Jillian. I want to have you again but it's too soon. I don't want to hurt you."

She looked up at him, her eyes full of wonder.

"I'm not allowed to say no to you."

He stared at her, unapologetic.

"No, you're not."

She looked away, then shyly lifted her luminous eyes to his.

"So I won't."

He moaned and rolled on top of her, taking her lips in an endless kiss. He made love to her again, slowly this time. It did hurt, but not nearly as much as the first time. And he brought her to climax twice. By dawn he'd taken her three more times, making her peak more times than she could count. She rolled over on his bed, thinking lazily that she might not mind being in service to the Prince so much after all.

PART TWO - JILLIAN

Jillian rolled over on the enormous bed, her body feeling heavy and tender. The light filtering in through the window made it look like late morning. She looked around the room and let it sink back in; she was at the Palace and she belonged to the Prince. It didn't seem as awful today, now that she knew how much she meant to him.

She smiled, remembering how fierce his green eyes had looked as he had plunged in and out of her again and again, making love to her as if his life depended on it.

Except the reality was, it was *her* life that depended on it. Her life and that of her entire family. Being selected as the Prince's Sofriquette was an enormous honor but also a heavy responsibility. She had to see to his pleasure, or else. Thankfully he hadn't expected her to actually 'do' anything. As a sheltered virgin, she had known less than nothing about how to please a man, let alone a Royal one.

She stretched and sat up, wondering what time it was. Her maids chose that exact moment to open the door. They were like cats, always appearing from nowhere.

They said nothing, just reaching for her and leading her to the bathing chamber.

Ouch. She was so sore between her legs it was difficult to walk.

"Wait- oh god-"

The maids glanced at her, knowing looks on their faces.

"Come Sofriquette, we will bathe you now. You are expected to join the Prince for meals. He already allowed you to skip breakfast."

She grimaced and let them pull her into the bathroom. 'Join' was the wrong word. She was to be displayed, always within his vision. The whole point was to keep him satisfied, and assured that his needs would be met at any time.

Jillian stepped into the pool as they guided her into the warm water. The water swirled around her legs, then higher, brushing against her apex. She screamed, jerking away. It felt like fire burning her between her legs. It hurt more than anything she'd ever experienced.

The maids looked at each other nervously, pushing her deeper into the water.

She was weeping as the water burned her most intimate spot. The maids soaped her up, rubbing between her legs as she sobbed.

"Hush Sofriquette. We will give you something to help with that."

They led her back to the table and guided her onto her back. Then they smoothed an unguent on her cleft. She immediately felt a cooling sensation. Claire, the head maid, was staring down at her, frowning.

"You are very irritated. Get some ice, Sabrina. And ask Valspar for some opiate."

One of the maids ran from the room as they continued to tend to her, rubbing oil into her flesh. They brushed her hair out and were applying her makeup as she lay there, still on her back. She looked up as Sabrina came back into the room.

She held a small brown bottle in one hand and an ice pack in the other.

Claire took the ice and laid it directly on Jillian's exposed sex. She flinched at the coolness, but the pain began to recede immediately.

"Oh... thank you."

Claire took a deep breath.

"Here, open your mouth."

"What is it?"

"It's a pain killer. It will help ease the discomfort. I'm afraid..."

"What?"

Jillian allowed Claire to dribble a few drops into her mouth. The taste was bitter but she immediately felt warmth spreading through her body. Ahhh...

"That's all I can give you right now I'm afraid. Any more will make you appear woozy. But I will leave this by your bedside. Once you are in bed, you can take more. Just don't be obvious about it."

Jillian nodded at Claire, liking the maid much better now. But Claire was frowning.

"Listen to me. You will have to take much more of this medicine. This pain will only get worse until you are allowed to heal. But there's no hope for it, he will want you again soon. I only wish he had gone gentler on you."

She snapped her mouth shut, realizing what she had just said. It sounded dangerously critical of the Prince. The maids all exchanged glances. Claire clapped her hands abruptly.

"Hurry!"

They removed the ice pack from her soft mound and sat her up. Then it was a flurry of dressing her hair, again lifting it high and back so that her face and throat were visible. Then they slipped pale silver underthings on her, the lace scratching her erect nipples. When Marie, the third maid, knelt before her to apply the honey to her lips she gasped, the light touch causing pain to rock through her once again.

The maids exchanged worried looks again but Jillian was too distracted to notice. Her nipples were so hard from the special cream they had applied. She wondered if she would ever get used to it.

They draped a silver dress over her body. It clung to her breasts and exposed the skin on her back, similar to the gown from the night before. It seemed even more erotic to be dressed this way during the day...

"Why are you preparing me this way now? Surely it can wait until dinner?"

The maids looked away from her, even Claire. They lifted the collar over her neck, locking it into place.

"You can be called to service at any time, Sofriquette. In fact..."

Jillian stared at the maid, realization dawning. She had said 'at any time.'

At any time.

"In fact, we were told to make you ready for this afternoon."

Oh god.

He was going to have her again. Soon. Of course he was. He had waited years apparently, unable to make love to anyone. The Royal penis being too precious to put just anywhere.

Of course he'd had some sort of instructor, he'd told her about this all last night. But he'd not made love until her, only observed. They'd both been innocents last night in a way. It had been intoxicating. If she wasn't so sore, she would want to climb back into bed with him again too.

She opened her eyes. Claire was staring at her.

"You can't tell him."

Jillian nodded. She knew that.

"Just take a few drops of the opiate. It will help. We will be back later to fit you for a new collar and wrist cuffs."

"Wrist cuffs?"

"Yes. The Prince wants a full set made. Wrists, ankles and waist."

"What for?"

Claire just shook her head.

"You'll see."

Jillian stood and waited just inside the door. After a few moments the knock came and the Prince stepped inside. He stepped forward and embraced her quickly.

"Hello my pet."

His warm voice tickled her ear. She smiled up at him as he stroked her face. He was so happy to see her. She could see the change in him. The Prince had always looked so serious, as if he had the weight of the world on his shoulders. Now he looked almost free.

He lifted the chain from his pocket and latched it to her collar. He ran the edge of his finger across her neck where the collar bit into her flesh.

"We'll replace this later today."

She nodded, her eyes on the gold chain as he let it run through his fingers.

"Come."

She fell into step behind the guards, taking the same route to the dining hall as yesterday. There was something going on up ahead, a commotion. She recognized the voice that was raised in anger.

Henry.

"Take her into the dining room, quickly."

She turned her head as they hurried through the great hall, seeing him there. Duke Henry was staring at her, his mouth agape. He took in her outfit as she froze, unable to take another step. His eyes flared as he noticed her nipples, barely covered by the flimsy dress she wore.

"Lady Jillian!"

He shouted and struggled against the guards who were holding him back.

Someone pulled on her chain sharply, making her look up. Valspar was pulling her forward, away from her former fiancé, away from the Prince who was striding across the room to his friend.

"Henry, be reasonable."

"You be reasonable! You could have any woman in the kingdom and you chose her?"

"Long before you did. Come, let's talk."

"There's nothing to talk about! You've made my fiance into your whore!"

The sound of a punch landing solidly against Henry's jaw was all she heard.

Jillian was seated with Sephina again. The whole room was silent as they waited for the Prince to join them. He came in a few minutes later, looking flushed. Everyone stood as he took the chain from Valspar and took his seat.

"How are you feeling today?"

Jillian was staring down at her plate, her emotions thrown into turmoil from Henry's outburst. The pain between her legs wasn't helping either. The cold, hard wood of the chair pressed into her softness cruelly.

She shook her head softly, unable to answer.

"I see. The Duke was the one you were to marry?"

She nodded softly.

"Did you love him?"

Jillian shook her head. She'd been fond of the Duke but they'd barely known each other. Last night had practically erased him from her mind, until now. She hated the pain she'd heard in his voice.

"Ah. That's good. I didn't think so, from the way you and his highness crackled and popped."

Jillian looked at the older woman, who was smiling slightly.

"I did not!"

Sephina only laughed.

"You did well last night, I can tell."

Jillian shot her another look. She was doing her best not to look at the Prince but she felt his eyes on her. Her cheeks were warm suddenly.

"How could you tell that? From the screaming match in the hallway?"

"No, I was at breakfast and the Prince looked happier than I've ever seen him."

Jillian swallowed. She wanted him to be happy... but she was in such turmoil.

"But you don't"

Jillian sipped the wine they brought her. She drank it swiftly, hoping it would settled her nerves.

"Something else is bothering you, I can tell."

"How do you do that?"

Jillian stared at Sephina with fond exasperation. The older woman smiled.

"Years of practice. Now tell me."

"Last night was... unexpected."

"Yes?"

"Yes. You were right. He doesn't hate me. He was... kind."

Sephina nodded.

"I knew he would be. So, what is wrong? You did not enjoy his lovemaking?"

Jillian finished her wine and another glass was immediately poured for her.

"No, I did. Much more than I thought I would. But-"

Sephina raised her eyebrow, waiting.

"Something is wrong now. I- I hurt."

The color drained from Sephina's face. That alone made Jillian's pulse race. Nothing so far had made the King's Sofriquette so much as blink.

"How many times did you make love last night?"

"Five times, I think. Maybe more. The last time went on for over an hour."

Sephina cursed under her breath.

"My dear, this is not good. He should have been more careful. A woman needs time to recover after making love, especially the first time."

"But what can I do?"

Sephina glanced at the Prince and groaned.

"I'm afraid you will have to risk his displeasure and tell him. He will be very disappointed but he won't want to harm you."

Jillian risked a peek at the Prince. He was gazing at her with sensual intent. She inhaled as his eyes drifted over her body. He was undressing her with his mind she could tell. Probably everyone in the room knew what he was doing. She felt warm all over and very, very alarmed.

Sephina had also noticed.

"Oh dear. I wish they would have let me instruct you. There are other ways to give him release and pleasure but you must know how."

"Can you tell me now? Please? I can't risk angering him."

Sephina shook her head sadly.

"There's no time. Look, he's already leaving."

She was right. The guards were there to collect her before lunch was even over. The Prince was staring at her, a hard look on his face. He was impatient to make love again.

Jillian followed the guards as they took the spiral staircase to her room, the Prince close behind her. At least they were going back to her chamber... maybe she could take more of that medicine...

She shivered, suddenly afraid. He didn't want to hurt her, he wouldn't do so deliberately she knew. But it was against the rules for her to say anything to dissuade him.

The guards opened her door and they stepped inside. The Prince frowned as her maids leapt forward with her new collar and cuffs.

"Shall we try these now your highness? We can adjust the size before dinner if need be?"

He nodded sharply and sat down, clearly annoyed. His eyes were on her as she stood stiffly, allowing them to place the new collar around her neck. It was wider, but it felt smoother against her throat, not as constricting. Next they knelt and attached matching cuffs to her ankles, snapping them into place. Then came a band that fit around her waist, this one with two loops on either side of her. Finally they slipped two bands over her wrists.

"How do they feel?"

Claire and the other maids were trying to hide their concern. It was useless to try and postpone the inevitable.

She tried to smile at them reassuringly but inside she felt only fear.

"Fine, thank you."

Jillian stared at her reflection in the mirror. She suddenly had a vision of herself, chained in any position he desired, awaiting his pleasure.

"Leave us."

"Shall we remove these first?"

"No."

The maids curtsied and left, Claire's eyes shifting to the bottle and back to Jillian's face. She nodded imperceptibly.

The moment the door closed Jillian's breath started to come faster, her chest rising and falling in fast little bursts. She knew what was coming. She knew-

"Come here Jillian."

She turned and walked toward him, her eyes lowered. He held his hand out and she took it, letting him guide her to his lap.

His hands wandered over her body as he sighed.

"I missed you this morning, but I thought I should let you sleep."

He nuzzled her neck, making her sigh with pleasure.

"You gave me great pleasure last night, little one."

His hands roved up to her breasts, opening her top so that they spilled out and into his eager hands. He moaned as he stroked her soft globes.

"I'm sorry you had to see that."

Her eyes lifted to his face, then lowered again. He was so much kinder than she ever imagined. Was it really possible she had so misunderstood him for all these years?

"I promised Henry many things today. I hate to see him suffer. I think he loved you."

She said nothing. What was there to say?

"I told him he could have any woman he wanted. I even offered to double his chosen bride's dower. I don't think he was pacified though."

His lips pressed against her temple as he inhaled her scent. She felt his manhood growing, pushing against her hip. Fear pooled in her stomach. If only she weren't so tender...

"I don't blame him of course. There's no woman alive who compares to you."

He kissed her, his tongue seeking deep in her mouth then withdrawing. It felt like- oh!

She felt her desire rising again. Her body responding to his, despite her discomfort. He groaned as he pressed his body against her.

"Come my pet. I would try out your new cuffs."

He stood and led her to the bed. She kept her eyes lowered so he would not see her fear. Perhaps it would be over quickly and he would let her rest. They could apply more ice. She could take- the medicine! She'd forgotten to take more. Her eyes darted to it as he pushed her toward the bed and onto her back.

He smiled at her sensuously as he opened a box by the bed. Gold chains lay inside, along with several locks and a key. He held the key up and grinned. Then he pulled one of the chains out and lifted her wrist, stringing the chain through the loop. There was a hook in the corner of the bed that she hadn't seen before. He guided the chain through the hook and tightened it, pulling her arm up and to the side. He clicked a lock into place, holding her securely. Then he moved down to her ankle.

He repeated the process with each leg and arm until she was spread eagle on the bed. She'd never felt so exposed in her life. She watched through hooded eyes as he undressed, his eyes never leaving hers. Then he climbed on top of her and started to undress her, slowly, as if unwrapping a gift.

His hands slid over every inch of her skin as it was exposed, making him moan. He ran his fingers up and down her thighs. Her hips circled. She was excited beyond belief, her desire mixing with the fear of what was to come. He leaned over her, kissing her mouth as he guided his shaft to her opening.

Oh god.

It hurt already. Just the lightest of touches burned her flesh. Then he slid forward, parting her plump lips. She closed her eyes tightly, grimacing. The pain was terrible and getting worse as he pushed deeper inside her tender slit.

She whimpered as he began to move inside her. His eyes were closed as her warmth surrounded him. He was lost in his pleasure, making small satisfied sounds in the back of his throat.

Tears were streaming down her face as he slid in and out of her without cease. Each stroke brought a fresh wave of pain. It felt as if her insides were scraped raw, without skin to protect her from his punishment.

He moved faster now, making her cry out again. He groaned, thinking she was moaning in pleasure. Her eyes turned to the side staring at the bottle of opiate, wishing she could take some. Maybe it would help-maybe-

He froze above her.

"Jillian?"

He had stopped moving, his shaft embedded deeply inside her.

"Look at me."

She closed her eyes and lifted them to his, unable to mask the tears of pain.

"My god, am I hurting you?"

She didn't answer him, just looked away. She was afraid.

He moaned in agony as he pulled himself out of her. He was staring down at her now, seeing how red her tiny cleft was.

"I was too rough with you- oh god. Why didn't you say anything to me, Jillian?"

She stared off to the side, the pain between her legs unbearable. Her eyes flickered to the bottle again.

"What are you looking at?"

He stood and strode over to the bedside table. He saw the bottle then and picked it up. He held it in front of her face.

"Is this what you want? What is this Jillian?"

He took her chin roughly and forced her to look at him. He was very, very angry. She whimpered, turning her head away.

"Be careful Jillian. That was very close to being a refusal."

She swallowed and forced herself to relax. She turned her head back and looked at him. He flinched when he saw her eyes. She was hurt and afraid.

"What is this? Who gave it to you?"

"The maids. It's- supposed to help with-"

She couldn't finish, the rage on his face making her close her eyes in fear. This was a man that was not to be trifled with. He closed his hand over the bottle convulsively. He face was a mask of disbelief.

"They knew you were hurt and they told you to drug yourself?"

She swallowed and nodded.

He closed his eyes and turned away from her, pulling his clothes back on.

He could barely look at her when he was done. He set the bottle back on the bedside table and pulled a blanket carelessly over her body, not looking at her.

Then he opened the door and stepped out. She heard his voice in the hallway.

"See to her."

Then he was gone.

Jillian didn't see the Prince for three days. She was on forced bed rest while she healed. Her maids waited on her hand and foot, bringing her food and books to pass the time. The Royal Physician was there at least three times a day to check on her progress.

She'd been shy at first but he'd assured her that he'd seen many beautiful naked women. The elderly doctor had teased her and made her laugh before he lifted the sheet to examine her. On the first day his eyes had looked concerned. He'd said little, only instructing her maids to reapply the ice once an hour and to keep her sedated.

On the second day he said she was healing nicely. They'd decreased her medicine and stopped using the ice.

On the third day the tenderness was almost gone completely. They had her laying on her back still though, refusing to let her rise. She was getting restless being immobile for so long.

But there was still no sign of the Prince. On the fourth day she was starting to worry that he was too angry to bear the sight of her. Perhaps he was already planning to rid himself of her. But she didn't truly believe that.

She lay on the bed, thinking about how he made her feel. She had time to think about her position and what it meant for the rest of her life... she could never marry. She couldn't even leave without his permission. And someday, she'd have to watch him marry another woman.

What would that be like? What about children? She longed to ask Sephina what she had done when the King married the Queen.

As if by magic her door opened and the King's Sofriquette slipped inside. She carried roses and a large wooden box.

"Don't get up!"

Jillian had been about to rise, to properly greet the older woman. Sephina sat on the edge of the bed, smiling widely at her young friend. Her blue gray eyes crinkled at her.

"Well, you've caused quite an uproar my dear."

"I have?"

Sephina nodded and handed her the box.

"From the Prince."

Then she lifted the roses.

"From me."

"Thank you."

Sephina merely smiled and looked around the room for a place to set her bouquet. She rose and walked toward the window, setting the flowers down on the small table there.

"The whole Palace has been on eggshells, trying to avoid the Prince. He's been in a foul temper for days. Well, go on, open it."

Jillian lifted the lid of the box. Inside were jewels. Lots and lots of jewels. There were emeralds, sapphires and rubies. But it was the enormous topaz necklace that caught her eye.

No wait- it was a headpiece, not dissimilar to a crown. Of course, she didn't need necklaces when she was the wear her collar at all times.

The golden stones were the exact shade of her own eyes. And the emeralds laying beside them matched the Prince's beautiful green eyes.

Sephina was laughing at the shocked expression on her face.

"I don't think he could chose so he just sent them all. You should have seen the jewelers face!"

Jillian swallowed. He hadn't forgotten her after all.

"I thought he was angry at me..."

"Oh, he was angry all right. But not at you."

Sephina stroked her hair softly.

"Never at you. I think things will change around here a bit, truth be told. No one will lay a finger on you again, that's for certain."

"He knows about that?"

Sephina nodded.

"It was a close call there. I thought he was going to order your maids to be executed when he heard about the rod."

Jillian's face went white. The maids had been especially gentle and subservient with her the past few days. Now she knew why.

"But he didn't of course. So, not to worry."

Jillian set the box aside and gathered her nerve.

"Sephina, can I ask you something?"

Sephina said nothing, just waiting.

"Do you- do you love the King?"

Sephina smiled.

"Of course. What devoted subject does not?"

Jillian rolled her eyes.

"You know that's not what I meant."

The woman simply smiled at her. Jillian realized she would not answer that question, maybe not ever. Perhaps that was an answer in and of itself.

"What is your question, really."

Jillian bit her lip.

"The Prince is to marry next year. My own marriage has just been called off. Now I will never be a wife. I'm somewhere in between. I can't imagine what that will be like, or how I will bear it..."

Sephina sighed and stood. She walked back and forth in front of the fire, gathering her thoughts.

"It's so different for you. No Sofriquette has ever been selected from the nobility before. There was quite a hullabaloo a few years ago when he made his choice. There was a long while they argued and made sure it was even legal!"

"There was?"

Sephina nodded.

"Oh yes. They tried to change the Prince's mind, parading lovely young things in front of him for months, but he would not be dissuaded."

"Oh."

That sent a warm rush of feelings through her. He had been awfully determined to have her. That had to count for something.

"I can't tell you how you will bear it my child. I was not to marry a Duke. I gave nothing like that up, other than the hope of having my own children."

Jillian raised her eyes to her.

"What do you mean? Are we not allowed to-"

"It's not so simple. We are fed food and drink to prevent contraception but there is no hard and fast rule against it. Of course, he must have a legitimate heir before he can have a bastard but it has been done. Many of our finest families are descended from Sofriquettes."

"Oh."

The word bastard hung heavily in the air.

"I don't envy you my child. Even in my position it was difficult to watch him marry another. To sit beside her in a way I never could. To bed her at night. He didn't want to at first. He often came to me before hand, to, um.. get him going."

Jillian's mouth was open, trying to imagine how that must have felt. She must have felt so used.

"But the Queen is a good woman. He grew to care for her. He cares for us both in different ways. For me it has always been enough."

She sat back down, and laid her hand over Jillian's.

"For your sake, I hope it can be enough for you too."

That evening the maids prepared her body carefully, following the same routine as they had before she was on bed rest. Instead of dressing her for dinner though, they slipped an elegant pink silk robe over her nude body and guided her to a chair. Soon servants were bustling into the room, carrying a table and laying it with plates and cutlery. They rolled in a cart piled high with food and drink, then withdrew.

A moment later, the Prince entered. He was dressed casually, his shirt partially unbuttoned, his hair still damp from bathing.

He looked so handsome he nearly took her breath away. She felt so shy as she stood and curtsied. He was staring at her when she rose. He looked... nervous.

He walked forward and took her hand, kissing it formally. Her eyes lifted to his face in surprise. This is how he used to greet her when they met in public. It brought back the feeling of unreality that she'd felt so many times since her change in position.

He'd always known though... each time he had seen her, or spoken to her, he'd had this arrangement in mind.

He smiled at her and sat in the chair opposite her. He poured them each a glass of wine from separate bottles. She wondered what was in hers this time... contraceptives no doubt. Did he also take an aphrodisiac?

"How are you feeling?"

He watched her face carefully as she answered.

"I'm fine, Your Highness. Truly."

He nodded, clearly relieved.

"I have been so worried and... sorry. I would never hurt you intentionally."

He looked so sad and earnest. She wanted to soothe him immediately. Even though the truth was that he held the power of life and death over her. She was sure now that he'd never use it, not matter how much she aggravated him.

"I know that. I never thought-"

Her voice trailed off as she stared awkwardly at her lap. She looked up and he was watching her with the softest look on his face.

"Come here Jillian."

She took a deep breath and stood, walking around the table to face him.

He moaned and pulled her onto his lap. His arms surrounded her, pulling her tightly against him as he kissed her.

"Hmmmm... so sweet..."

He kissed her for a while, his hands softly stroking her back. She felt his manhood rising against her and smiled. But he just held her there for a few minutes before carrying her back to her chair.

He strolled over the rolling cart and smiled at her over his shoulder.

"I think we are supposed to serve ourselves..."

She stood.

"I will do it, Your Highness."

"No! You sit!"

He gave her a stern look before turning his attention to the cart, lifting a cover to reveal a small salad.

"I think that's mine."

He stared at her, not understanding.

"I'm on a strict diet."

"But that's ridiculous! You are perfect just as you are!"

She smiled.

"I think it has more to do with other things actually."

"Go on."

"Sephina told me that our food is liberally dosed with aphrodisiacs and contraceptives."

His mouth opened. He didn't know... interesting. He looked intrigued, though.

"Do they work?"

"What, your highness?"

"The aphrodisiacs."

She smiled at him, shrugging.

"I don't know. They do apply something to my skin that makes it extra sensitive."

He closed his eyes and moaned, obviously aroused by the thought.

"They always apply extra to me here... and here..."

She was teasing him now, her hand sliding up to cup on breast, and then the other, lightly circling her nipples through her robe. What had gotten into her?

He was staring at her, his mouth agape. He looked like he wanted to pounce on her. But he didn't move.

"Jillian..."

She looked up at him, her fingers still circling lightly over her breasts.

"Yes, Your Highness?"

"Please... oh god... don't do that. I don't want to hurt you..."

Ohhhh... so that was it.

She stood and walked toward him. He was staring at her as if she were the devil incarnate. His eyes slid down her body and he closed them, willing himself to look away. She slid her hands up over his chest, feeling his muscles jump under her fingers.

"You won't."

His eyes snapped open. He stared down at her urgently.

"You're sure?"

She nodded and he was on her so quickly she would have missed it if she blinked. His hand yanked her up against him as he kissed her deeply. He was like a starving man who had unexpectedly been given a banquet. He scooped her up and carried her to the bed, laying her down and undressing quickly.

She stared up at him, desire radiating from her face.

"Shall I put on my cuffs, your highness?"

He moaned and reached for her robe, tearing it open. He was on top of her instantly, his warm body pressing her into the bed. He kissed her and let his mouth slide to her ear.

"Later."

A thrill went through her at his word, and the unspoken promise there. She knew he wouldn't hurt her. And she wanted to feel him inside her... the sooner the better.

"Ohhh..."

His mouth was on her breasts, licking and sucking frantically. Then he slid down, his mouth closing over her soft cleft. He kissed her tenderly, slowly, using all his skill to drive her wild. He made little nibbling kisses all over her bare skin. Every touch made her more sensitive. She wiggled, wanting more.

He chuckled as she rocked her hips helplessly, then slid his tongue between her plump lips. Again and again he drove his tongue into her, making her cry out and writhe on the bed. She was so close to her peak- she was-

"Oh, oh, oh, oh, OH!"

She leapt off the bed, her hips bucking her body against his mouth. He moaned, clearly loving it as she climaxed. He used his fingers to lightly stroke her nipples as he slid his tongue up and down her slit, prolonging her orgasm endlessly.

Finally he lifted his head and looked at her. She was looking at him with pure adoration and trust. He could have done anything to her at that moment and she wouldn't have complained.

He saw the look in her eyes and froze. Then he unleashed his passion on her, guiding his shaft to her cleft and driving in. He worked his manhood deep into her opening insistently. But also gently.

He pumped himself into her for a long while, pausing every time one of them came close. He wanted to make this last, that much was obvious.

She was whimpering as he made love to her, teasing her, denying them both. Her nipples were stimulated with every stroke as his chest rubbed against them, again and again.

He was watching her face as he slid a hand between their bodies and softly circled his finger on her sensitive nub, making her gasp.

"Oh!"

He smiled grimly, holding himself back. He made long slow thrusts into her as his fingers dancing over her, faster and faster.

She was going to climax she realized. It was about to happen and it was going to be *big*.

Her hips jerked against him. If he hadn't been on top of her, holding her down with his shaft, she would have flown through the air. The force of her orgasm was that great. He moaned as she convulsed around him. He threw his head back and unleashed, finally allowing himself to pour himself into her, taking his pleasure.

She felt his shaft pulse as he exploded inside her. His heat filled her up, warming her with his seed. Her body grasped at him instinctively, pulling him deeper inside her.

They both moaned in ecstasy as they held still, trying to regain their breath.

Finally she opened her eyes to find him staring down at her tenderly. He kissed her and lifted his body up. He stood and started pulling on his clothes quickly. When he was dressed he kissed her again. Then he pulled away with an effort and smiled.

"Enjoy your dinner. Please promise me you will more than the salad."

She nodded her agreement. And he was gone.

The next few days developed into a pattern. The Prince escorted her to meals and then made love to her just once immediately after dinner and then left. Each time he labored over her endlessly, making it last, bringing her to climax again and again. After the first night where he took her five times, she was starting to wonder what was wrong.

Finally, after almost a week of this, she asked Sephina what she thought during lunch.

The older woman was eating a berry as she pondered how to answer her.

"You really don't know?"

Jillian shook her head softly.

"Has he tired of me?"

The Sofriquette laughed.

"Have you looked at him lately? He looks like a general going into battle."

Jillian stole a look at the Prince. He had been watching her constantly, as usual. Right now he was grimly staring into the space below her collarbone. She turned away just as his gaze slipped back to her face.

"He does look... intense."

"He's waging a war with himself. Desire and control. You said he leaves you every night, after you make love?"

"Yes, but only once. I know it's not my place to ask him to stay..."

"True but there are other ways. You could always ask him to teach you something else."

"Like what?"

"Has he ever pleasured you with his mouth?"

Jillian blushed hotly and looked away. She ended up catching the Prince's eye at that moment. He was studying her hotly. It was as if he knew what she was thinking. She looked down and nodded.

"Well, we can do that for them too."

"We can? But it's so-"

"Hmmm... perhaps I can give you a small lesson this afternoon. Would you like that? It can be our little secret."

Jillian nodded eagerly. She realized that she wanted nothing more that to please him, and to be pleased by him. She would try anything the Sofriquette suggested.

"Very well. I'll come to your room in an hour."

They smiled at each other. Jillian counted herself lucky to have the older woman as a friend.

The Prince had walked her to her room again after lunch. She felt him hesitate before he took his leave. He had things to do she was sure, but he had wanted to come inside. He looked a bit cranky as he walked away from her door. Wasn't the whole point to keep him from getting distracted?

She walked around her chamber, waiting for Sephina. She was bored she realized. Was she allowed to do anything but wait for his pleasure? It wouldn't so bad, if he was actually taking her up on her constant availability!

Jillian stopped in her tracks, staring out the window. Did she just admit to herself that she wanted to be used? To be taken without a word?

Oh god, she did. Not by just anyone of course. She wanted *him*. She was falling in love with the Prince.

She sunk to the window seat, her hands covering her face.

That's when Sephina knocked softly and opened the door. She held a basket, covered with a piece of cloth. It hid the contents from prying eyes. Jillian tried to put her thoughts from her mind. She was instantly curious about what was in the basket.

Sephina raised her eyebrows in unspoken question. The older woman could tell something was bothering her. It didn't bother Jillian that she read her like a book. But they'd already gotten adept at silent communication. So when Jillian shook her head, Sephina didn't press her for an answer.

"Come in, come in!"

The maids had put out plates of fruit and two glasses with herbed wine. They clinked their glasses together and drank. Jillian peered into her glass comically, wondering as always what was in it. Sephina laughed.

She pulled Jillian to the pillows in front of the fire and sat, putting the basket between them.

"Go ahead."

Jillian lifted the cloth that concealed the contents of the basket. She peeled it back to reveal... bananas. There were bananas inside. Also what looked like a lollipop and something else- oh.

A glass sculpture of a- oh my! It was a phallus and it looked a lot like the Prince's manhood... in fact...

"It's an exact replica. Well, more or less. I'm told he refused to sit still long enough to get a proper mold."

Sephina was laughing at the shocked look on Jillian's face.

"We'll get to that later. First let's have a look at the banana. It's good place to start because it's so tender and you have to mind your teeth."

That evening as the maids prepared her for dinner, Jillian was busy mentally reviewing everything Sephina had shown her. They covered her in a dress made of dark gleaming bronze, then placed her new collar around her throat. The topaz headpiece was worked into her elaborate hairstyle.

An image of the Sofriquette kneeling before the King came to her unbidden. The King's face was relaxed, awash in pleasure as the dark haired woman worked her head on his shaft.

Oh my.

She didn't want to think about that. It didn't seem right to think of their monarch that way. Much better to think about the Prince, his head thrown back, as she knelt before him... hmmmm. Maybe she would get the hang of this 'object of desire' thing after all. Then again, she had a lot of conflicting feelings. It had barely been a little longer than a week since she'd been a pampered young woman of the upper class.

Now she was the pampered pet of the future King. She had very few of the freedoms she had taken for granted before. But in a way, she had much greater power. It was a strange twist of fate to be sure.

The door opened and she greeted the Prince. He stared at her hungrily, as if he would skip the meal altogether. She smiled, thinking that the meal she had planned would consist of *him*.

He clipped the gold chain onto her collar as she let her eyes rest on his groin. She could have sworn she saw it grow under her gaze... she looked up and caught the look of frustrated desire on his face. She turned and followed the guards in their procession, letting her hips sway under the revealing gown.

She was quiet during the meal, sharing secretive smiles with Sephina. Every time she looked up the Prince looked more and more frustrated. It was a good thing she had a new trick up her sleeve because he looked like he might burst if he had to have her only once again that night. Then again, she also meant to make sure he knew that he could have her twice or three times without hurting her. They just couldn't go for five again anytime soon. That had to be some kind of a record.

The meal seemed to drag on as she sipped her wine. Inside she felt warm but her skin was cool. She wished she had something to cover her, and not just for modesty's sake. It was shocking how quickly the desire to cover her body had dissipated. She hardly even noticed that her hard nipples attracted the gaze of every man in the castle. She almost pitied the guards who tried the hardest to hide their stares. She was displayed to arouse desire, to be available for the Prince's viewing pleasure. She could hardly blame them for noticing.

Finally she found herself back inside her chamber. The Prince stepped inside behind her, his eyes hot on her body. She melted into his embrace, feeling his turgid shaft pressing against her. He started licking her neck as if he would devour her. His hands were at her hips immediately, pulling her mound against him rhythmically. She sensed his urgency to be inside her.

"Am I permitted to have desires of my own?"

Her whisper sounded tentative to her ears. She hoped her plan would work... He stopped what he was doing, lifting his mouth from her neck. He swallowed and nodded, watching her eyes carefully for a clue as to what she was after.

She slid down his body as he watched intently. His eyes widened as she knelt before him.

"I want to taste you your highness."

She slid her hands up and over him, caressing him through his pants. He closed his eyes in indecision.

"You give me so much pleasure when you kiss me there... can I not give you some pleasure in return?"

He moaned and opened his eyes, his hand shifting to his pants, pulling them apart. His member sprang free and she grasped it, guiding it to her lips. Her tongue snaked out and twisted around the head as she pulled him gently into her mouth. He moaned helplessly, already losing control. His warm hands tangled in her hair.

She held the base of his engorged manhood with one hand as she sunk her soft lips over him, taking him deeper into her warm mouth. Then she began the rhythm that Sephina had taught her. Bobbing her head slowly on his shaft, twisting slightly with each stroke. He was gasping for air as she increased the pressure of her hands and lips and increased the tempo.

His hands were gripping her head now, allowing him to insert his rod deeper into her throat. She gagged slightly as he pumped into her mouth. She covered her teeth with her lips and worked her tongue along the base of his cock, making him moan in ecstasy.

Down on her knees, she suddenly felt a sense of power unlike she had ever known. The Prince was beyond himself, totally under her control. And this was a skill she would only improve at.

His body was shaking as he stroked his member into her eager mouth, pressing into her again and again.

Finally he froze and a warm liquid erupted from his cock head. It tasted salty and strange in her mouth but she swallowed it quickly. Sephina had been very specific about this part. Her tongue danced over the tip of his shaft as it spurted jets of his seed into her mouth.

His hands loosened their grip on her head as the last of his juices were released. She suckled him for a moment longer, then licked his tip once more before leaning back on her heels. He was looking down at her with a look of pure awe. He took her hand and lifted her into his arms.

"My god Jillian..."

She smiled as he cuddled her. Then she went to get them each a glass of wine. Tonight there was only one bottle. She looked at him questioningly.

"I thought we could share the same vintage tonight."

She lowered her eyes, wondering if the aphrodisiac was in this bottle. They would be in for quite a night if so...

Hours later she wasn't sure if it was Sephina's advice, or the wine but they had reached a new level of lovemaking. He had taken her again, making love to her tenderly. Before he could dress, she had rolled on top of him and straddled his hips.

"I'll never tell you what to do, but you don't have to go..."

He moaned and grasped her breasts as she arched her back above him.

"Are you sure? I don't want to-"

"Yes, your highness. I'm sure."

They had made love again, with her on top, finishing with her beneath him once again. He had fallen asleep then, tangled in her arms. She was drifting off herself when she heard the furtive noise coming from the window. Someone was in the room.

"Well, well, not so reluctant after all."

She opened her eyes to see the blade pointed directly at her heart.

Henry.

PART THREE - JILLIAN

Henry's eyes swept over her naked body with contempt. Not just contempt... there was also hot lust. Jillian felt heat on her skin as his eyes slid down her body. He was staring hungrily at her bare cleft when the Prince opened his eyes.

Jillian felt him stiffen, his hands instinctively clutching her naked body where she tangled with him. It was barely dawn and they'd been sleeping when the Duke, her former fiancé, had broken into her chamber. He had a razor sharp sword clutched in his hand.

"Get up, whore."

Henry was looking at her face now, sneering. She couldn't help it, she whimpered in fear.

"Don't move, Jillian."

The Prince was tensing, trying to position himself in front of her but the Duke was too fast.

Henry stepped forward, his blade pointed at her throat, touching her skin. Jillian's whole body started to shake.

"Get up or I will cut you."

She closed her eyes tightly, the Prince's hands closed like manacles around her.

"And then I'll cut him."

The Prince inhaled sharply. Everything Duke Henry was doing was treasonous, but threatening a Royal was immediately punishable by death.

"Leave now and I will let you live Henry. We can forget all about this."

Henry laughed bitterly, letting his sword slide down Jillian's body, the sharp cold point digging into her flesh. He tilted his head to the side, licking his lips.

"Forget that you stole my bride? Turned her into this trollop... it *is* quite a display I must say. What a delightful bed partner you must be."

Jillian stared at him as he licked his lips grotesquely.

"Don't hurt her Henry."

He looked away from her body finally, staring at the Prince.

"Please."

Henry's eyebrows shot up. Then he threw his head back and laughed. He slid his hand onto Jillian's arm and started pulling her away from the Prince, out of the bed.

"No!"

The Prince was forced to let go as the sword pressed into her tender flesh. He watched in horror as Henry held Jillian against him, his hand splayed over her belly.

She stared into the Prince's eyes in utter terror, begging him to stay put, not to move...

"I'm not going to hurt her. I'm just going to fuck her. I'm going to fuck her *a lot*."

His tongue lapped at the side of her face. She cringed away from him, disgusted.

The Prince's eyes flared.

"You know I can't allow that Henry."

"Oh that's right, if someone else contaminates your precious harlot, you can't have her anymore. Isn't that right?"

Jillian whimpered as Henry's hand slid up, cupping her breast and squeezing it painfully.

"Please Henry. I'll give you anything you want. Just ask."

"I want her. And now I've got her. Making you suffer is just an added bonus."

Jillian felt herself starting to faint, her body slipping in Henry's grasp as he held the blade to her throat. The Prince was reaching for her, a desperate look in his eyes.

"Henry. I am begging you. Please... I love her."

The words barely permeated the haze of fear Jillian was in. She started to fall forward, causing Henry to yank her roughly up again. His blade nicked her throat, causing a trickle of blood to dribble down her chest. She moaned.

"That's unfortunate but as you said, unavoidable. Don't worry, I'll send her back with my baby in her belly in a couple of months."

He laughed again and started dragging her backwards toward the window. Jillian felt him pushing her onto the ledge outside. She realized that she was nude and two stories up. Anyone standing in the courtyard could see her clearly.

Her eyes opened finally, registering shock as he pushed her closer to the edge. She knew that her life was over. She stared at the Prince, looking deeply into his anguished eyes. And then she fell.

Faint sounds of revelry greeted Jillian when she woke. Her entire body was sore. She tried to stretch before realizing she couldn't move. She was tied to a wooden chair, sitting up. Her arms were pulled back behind her cruelly and her legs were spread, each tied to the outside of the chair legs with a rough and scratchy rope that scraped her skin cruelly. She moaned around the gag in her mouth.

She must be in a private room at a tavern she thought, straining to regain her sense of equilibrium. The sounds coming from below confirmed her suspicion. She heard gulls and the faint smell of the ocean drew her attention. A tavern near the wharf. Henry must be planning to escape by ship on the eastern sea. With her.

Henry.

She lifted her head, scanning the shadows of the room. There was someone there, in the shadows. He was lounging in a deep chair, his booted feet on a table. There was a tankard of something clasped in his fist. He pulled on it deeply then dropped the empty cup to the floor where it rolled across the room.

"Sleeping beauty is awake at last."

His words sounded slurred as he dropped his feet heavily to the floor. He stood and walked toward her, coming into the light. Her eyes were adjusting so she could see him. She could see the look on his face.

"I thought about defiling you while you slept but I decided I wanted to see your eyes. More fun that way, don't you think?"

She whimpered pitifully. He grinned at her cruelly and reached out, pulling down the sheet he'd partially covered her body with. Her nipples pointed obscenely into the air. She wasn't sure if it was the cold or the stimulant cream that was doing it.

He inhaled sharply and ran his hands over her breasts. She tried to speak to him through the gag, to get his attention, to make him stop. Her eyes searched his face but his gaze was intent on her body. He concentrated deeply as he massaged her round breasts again and again. Then he frowned, seeming to come out of his daze.

His eyes looked to hers. There was an accusation there.

"You were supposed to be mine."

She tried to reason with him but the gag muffled her words. He pulled a knife out of his boot and fingered it, considering. He reached for the gag in her mouth.

"Don't scream."

Jillian nodded her head, desperate to try... maybe she could make him listen to reason. He pulled it down around her throat.

"Please, Henry. Please... let me go. You don't want to do this..."

He frowned at her again, confusion dimming his blue eyes. She had once thought those eyes were so fine, so noble. He had no honor now. She closed her eyes, knowing she had to hide her disgust from him if she was to survive this.

"You must be thirsty."

He looked around, realizing he was out of ale. He unlocked the door and shouted down.

"More ale!"

Then he stood at the door, staring at her. Tears were in her eyes as she considered her predicament. If he touched her. If he invaded her body... she could no longer be with the Prince. That thought filled her with despair. She loved him. There was no point in denying it to herself any longer.

A servant brought two tankards of ale to the door, staring at her naked body in surprise. She tried to gesture to him but he was looking at her cleft, her legs spread obscenely by the rope. The sheet had slipped completely, revealing every inch of her. Henry handed the man some coin and clapped him on the back.

"What a beauty! Send her around when you're finished will you?"

"If there's anything left. I like my whores tied up."

The man laughed and left the room, giving her body a last long look and rubbing his groin. Jillian forced herself to breath as Henry approached her with the ale. He poured a good portion of one tankard down his gullet before reaching for her head. He tilted her chin back and made her swallow the bitter ale. She choked on it, tears streaming down her face now.

Henry stared down at her, a bulge growing by the second in his pants. His hand stroked the tears from her face tenderly. The gentleness of his hand made everything else he was doing so much worse. He was capable of kindness, even in his deranged state.

Why was he doing this to her?

"Henry, please. You don't have to do this. You could run and he would let you go. He cares for you. He'll forgive you."

A snarl crossed Henry's face as he leaned down, inches from her.

"Well, I don't forgive him!"

He grabbed her head and kissed her roughly, bruising her lips. Then his hand was at his buckle, removing his belt, shifting his pants down to reveal his engorged cock. It was long and heavily veined. It looked so pink and disgusting compared to the Prince's member.

She whimpered and tried to move away as he adjusted her body on the chair. He dragged her hips to the edge of the seat and spread her legs painfully, pushing them even further out to the sides.

"No!"

His hands were on her thighs as he stared down at his shaft when the door banged open. Guards swarmed the room as the Prince ran in and threw Henry off of her. His eyes were full of despair as he looked into her eyes. He covered her with his cloak and untied her as she wept. Her tears were of relief.

"Shhhh... it's alright. You're safe now, my love."

He scooped her up into his arms, carrying her from the room. She heard Henry shouting incoherently behind her. The Prince carried her outside and into a carriage where he tenderly held her close, the entire journey back to the castle.

She clung to his chest as he stroked her back, warming her.

"You were very brave, Jillian."

"I was so afraid. I tried to reason with him but he-"

The Prince stiffened.

"Shhhh... it's alright. I have to ask you Jillian. Did he-"

"No."

He squeezed her tightly.

"You can tell me. I won't send you away. I don't care about the stupid rules!"

She breathed deeply.

"He didn't. He was about to but he was so drunk. It made him move slowly."

He kissed her forehead.

"Did he hurt you?"

"No, he just looked at me. He kissed me and he touched me- on my chest- but that's all."

"I'm so sorry Jillian. I never thought he would do something like that. I guess I never knew him at all."

"Me either. What will- happen to him?"

"He'll be tried and most likely executed. I'm so sorry Jillian. I wish none of this had happened..."

She turned her face into his shoulder and wept.

The Prince waited in her room while her maids bathed her, unwilling to leave her side. The Royal Physician came and looked her over, prescribing rest and opiate for the bruises around her wrists and ankles. The mark on her throat where Henry had cut her would leave a scar but there was nothing that could be done about it. The best they could do was treat it to prevent infection.

Finally they were alone. The Prince was feeding her a warm broth that seemed to make her sleepier by the minute.

"May I ask you a question?"

He stopped feeding her and nodded his assent.

"What is it Jillian?"

"I don't understand something."

He raised his eyebrows, lifting the spoon to her lips. She swallowed the broth.

"How did we get down from the window? I thought that surely I was about to-"

"Shhhh..."

The Prince lifted another spoonful to her lips, cutting off the unwelcome thought. She opened her mouth obediently. He sighed.

"Henry had men waiting outside. They caught you."

"Oh."

She blushed, realizing she had been nude. He held the spoon up again.

"I'm not hungry."

"Eat."

His look made it clear that this was a direct order. She opened her mouth again, allowing him to feed her the rest of the broth.

"You will rest now. Lay down."

She scooted down into the big bed. He kissed her forehead then stood and checked the window. Her eyes were growing heavy as she saw him take a seat by the fireplace. She woke briefly in the night and he was still there, staring into the flames. There was a pensive look on his face, as if he were grappling with a terrible problem. She wondered what it was before she once again drifted into unconsciousness.

The next day she was again confined to her room. There were workmen at her window early in the morning, affixing bars. It made her chamber feel like a prison, which in a way, it was. She'd managed to delude herself about that until now...

She paced around the room and nibbled at her breakfast. The doctor came to see her again before lunch. Her maids had yet to appear to bath or change her so she sat in her robe, staring out of the window.

When her lunch came on a rolling cart, her eyes widened. It was a huge meal, several platters full. She was not surprised when the Prince came in to join her. He looked tired as he kissed her.

He sat down and patted his knee. Jillian blushed as she sat on his lap. She wasn't sure she would get used to being treated like a treasured pet. It was nice to be held in his arms though. He fed her slowly, growling when she licked the food off of his fingers.

"You aren't hungry?"

"I already ate."

"Oh."

He held another forkful of fish to her lips.

"Open."

"I'm stuffed! They'll have to roll me into the dining room tonight!"

He smiled grimly and held the fork to her lips. She opened her mouth taking the food. He fed her a few more bites just to be perverse. She felt herself growing sleepy as he cradled her against his chest.

"I have to go away for a few days."

"What?"

"I would give anything for it not to be now."

"Am I to go with you?"

He squeezed her tightly.

"Not this time, little one."

She yawned and snuggled deeper into his shoulder.

"Where are you going?"

He stroked her back and laid a kiss on her soft hair.

"That I cannot tell you."

The Prince left early the next morning. He came to say goodbye, kissing her deeply and staring at her as if he were afraid he might never see her again.

Something was obviously wrong but she knew better than to ask him what it was. He hadn't made love to her the night before. She knew it was because of her ordeal but she couldn't help it. She wished he had taken her again and again. She would miss him. She would miss his touch.

She had little to do over the next week. She took all her meals in her room. Sephina came to take her for a walk once a day, but other than that she was alone. Most of the time she slept. They must be putting something in her food...

On the fourth morning she was surprised to hear a familiar voice in the hallway.

Her mother.

The door opened and she stared at her beautiful mother. She had always looked up to Lady Danielle. Her mother was a cold and haughty noblewoman who never had a hair out of place, and rarely a kind word for her daughter.

Her eyes were curious as she looked at her daughter. Removed. Jillian knew she must be disappointed that her daughter was no longer to become a Duchess. With a pang she realized she hadn't even asked what had happened to Duke Henry. Perhaps it was better not to know.

"Please come in, mother. Sit."

Her mother was staring at her as she took her seat. It was hard not to notice that Jillian was dressed to display her femininity. Her skin was freshly oiled and her eyes lined with kohl.

"You are well, Jillian?"

"Yes thank you. And yourself? Father?"

Her mother nodded, accepting a glass of wine from one of the maids. There were two separate vessels as usual. Jillian was handed another glass. She wondered if it was laced with sedatives again. Obviously they were drugging her. She wondered if she'd ever get used to it.

"We are well thank you."

Jillian smiled demurely and looked at her lap. There must be a reason for this visit. Her mother was nothing if not calculating.

"My dear, we wanted to discuss with you the situation with Haight. As you know, your father has business dealings there. It is of utmost importance that you be as circumspect as possible regarding the new Princess."

Jillian stared at her mother in shock. What was she talking about?

"You didn't know? Surely they must have prepared you..."

Jillian shook her head, dread pooling in her stomach.

"The Prince has gone to Haight to formalize the marriage contract. The wedding is in two weeks."

The floor seemed to drop out from under Jillian. She had known this would happen but it was too soon... oh god.

"There is a war brewing in the South. The Haight's need our support so they requested the wedding take place now instead of next year as originally planned. My dear, you knew this was to happen. Does it really matter when?"

Jillian shook her head. She refused to show her mother how much the words hurt. Her mother sighed.

"We had such high hopes for you my dear. Still, your position can be of some use to us. So long as you remain unobtrusive. They have different values in Haight. I doubt the Princess will be pleased to have you paraded in front of her."

This was worse than Jillian could have anticipated. The jealousy was overwhelming her, making her body feel like it was on fire. And there was a new feeling... shame.

"Well, it's good to see you looking well. I trust we can count on you to be wise? You will do as we ask?"

Jillian nodded jerkily.

"Yes, of course mother."

Lady Danielle stood and kissed her daughter's head softly.

"Your father and brother send their love."

Jillian curtsied as her mother took her leave. The door closed behind her and she sunk to the floor. She was too upset to cry. Her whole body felt like it was made of lead.

He was getting married.

It was three more days before the Prince returned. She slept much of the days, tossing and turning at night.

Finally she was given an even stronger sleeping draught to help her sleep. The next morning when she woke, she knew instantly she wasn't alone in the room.

Prince Maximilian was sitting in a chair near the fireplace. He was watching her sleep, a hooded look on his face. Jillian sat up slowly. She felt warmth flood her chest. She was glad to see him, despite everything.

He smiled when he saw the soft look on her face.

"Come here, sleeping beauty."

She flinched, remembering that Henry had called her that. The Prince didn't notice. His eyes were on her body... he wanted her...

She stood and walked slowly toward him. Her thin sleeping gown was designed to show her lithe figure to its best advantage. Sheer lace panels cut into the sides and down the center of her body, revealing her

145

flat stomach, barely concealing any part of her. His eyes flared as he gazed at her body hungrily. She felt herself responding, before they even touched. He was watching her face as he pulled her into his lap.

He kissed her deeply, with something that felt like desperation. His arms closed around her and Jillian forgot for a moment that he was to marry another. But only for a moment.

She closed her eyes as he slipped her nightgown off her shoulders and began kissing her softly. He trailed kisses down her neck and across her collarbone, finally taking one of her nipples into his mouth. He moaned as he swirled his tongue around the hard nub. Jillian arched her back, sighing softly.

He lavished her breasts with attention endlessly, making her rock her hips against him restlessly. Finally he lifted his head to stare down at her. His hands roved over her back and hips. Jillian felt his arousal pressing against her insistently. She wanted him. It was no longer an obligation. *She wanted him.*

Whore.

That's what she was. That's how his bride would see her. She was his whore.

He froze as he saw the look of shame on her face.

"Jillian."

She closed her eyes.

"Who told you?"

She took a deep breath, trying to regain control of her emotions. He squeezed her hips, demanding her attention and obedience.

"Jillian, look at me. You will answer me."

She lifted her eyes to his.

"Answer me!"

"My mother."

He cursed under his breath and stood, carrying her to the bed. He laid her down and crossed the room, pouring himself a glass of wine. He poured her a glass from her own decanter as well. She took it and hesitated before she drank.

"What is it?"

"There's something new they've been giving me. A sedative I think."

He stared at her. He hadn't known... they were both at the mercy of the King's advisor in their ways.

"Drink mine then."

"It's fine."

She swallowed her wine quickly. Perhaps it was better to be sedated. Perhaps it would ease the humiliation.

"You are very close to disobeying a direct order."

She looked at him in alarm. He was upset. *Very upset.* He was staring at her with anger. She hadn't meant to push him.

"You'd rather be numb that be with me? Is that it Jillian? I'm not sure I would blame you."

"No! Never... I swear."

She sat up on the bed and pulled her slip over her head.

"Can we- can we just pretend that none of this is happening? Please, Your Highness..."

He crossed the room in an instant, wrapping his arms around her. He grabbed her face and stared into her eyes, sorrow and desire radiating out of him in waves. Her eyes filled with tears but she refused to let even one spill onto her cheeks.

He loved her. She knew it. No matter what else happened she knew that he loved her back. She felt it in her bones.

He kissed her then. Ever fiber of her being felt his worship as he tasted and soothed her. He pressed her backwards onto the bed and began making love to her. He lingered over her endlessly, caressing, tasting. He made her climax with his mouth and fingers over and over. She begged him to take her but he only shushed her, lowering his head to her apex again.

Finally he pulled his body up, pressing his shaft against her apex.

"You're mine Jillian. You belong to me. Say it."

"Yes. I'm yours."

He drove into her sheath, his body filling her with his warmth.

"Forever."

"Forever."

He plunged into her again and again, making her cry out again with her release. He didn't tarry this time. He let himself go, taking his pleasure from her willing flesh.

He stared into her eyes as he shuddered, his seed filling her belly. He held her in his arms, still deep inside her. Then he took her again.

Jillian nearly forgot the truth under the tender siege he laid upon her that day and for the next nine. Nearly, but not quite.

In ten days, his bride would come.

PART FOUR - MAXIMILLION

Prince Maximilian stood with his father and mother, waiting to greet his bride. His mother smiled at him sympathetically. He felt sick to his stomach if the truth were known. Anyone who knew him well, knew that he dreaded this.

Because of her.

Jillian.

His beautiful concubine. She was all he could think about. He'd selected her years ago, one woman from amongst all the women in the Kingdom. She was a high born noblewoman.

In the past all the chosen had been pretty peasant girls or the daughters of a merchants. He'd been encouraged to look over some women from the lower classes and he'd agreed, just to pacify his father the King. But it was inevitable. It had to be her.

Growing up they'd often been thrown into contact. He was the Prince and she was the daughter of an Earl. Spoiled and beautiful, always knowing that she was adored. That she'd always be adored. When her family had finally mentioned her betrothal to the King's advisor, it had been time to take action.

She had fought him. Once she'd been plucked from her former life and informed of her new responsibilities. Not overtly, she couldn't do that without risking her life or the lives of her family. But he had sensed her anger, her outrage at being forced to serve him.

He had rejoiced the first time he saw her in her collar, the first time he locked the chain into place. Not that he'd ever used it. The chain was symbolic, like the collar. It was just a reminder to all that she belonged to him. It was a reminder *to her*.

From the moment he'd known that he would want a woman someday, he'd known it would be her. Usually the Royal Concubine was selected from the farming class. One pretty and intelligent peasant girl was selected to rise to the highest position, the King's mistress, to ease and comfort him with her body. But he'd bucked tradition and chosen a noblewoman. One who was about to marry his former friend, Duke Henry.

All the same, he hadn't hesitated. Not for a second.

The Prince could admit that it had given him pleasure to master her, to tame the girl who had tossed her head at him so many times, singeing him with her fiery eyes. She had never been the type to suck up. But now, she didn't have a choice. Both her life and that of her entire families' rested in his grasp.

He knew it was unfair but he didn't care. He reveled in watching her fight her instincts, watching her bend to his will. It hadn't been easy but eventually she had bent, surprisingly so. As soon as she'd surrendered, he found that he had as well.

He'd found passion in her arms and pleasure beyond his wildest imaginings. She was a fierce contradiction of innocence and passion. He was driven to seek her bed again and again. And she had no choice but to accept him. He knew that. He knew it wasn't just. But he did it anyway.

Last night he had kept them both up until the dawn, taking her again and again. He was always careful not to hurt her, not after the first time when he'd let his eager body override his common sense. But last night had been different. They had been desperate for each other, moving together like a machine whose engine was fueled by fear.

They hadn't spoken of today. Of the arrival of his bride. But they had both been keenly aware of the significance of today.

Now she was inside, locked in her chamber. Normally he would have her with him, the slender gold chain that bound them wrapped around his hand. She was his. But the King's advisor had decided it was better to keep her out of sight for now.

Her carriage arrived. Letticia, Princess of Haight. He'd met her before, at the betrothal, though they had barely spoken a word to each other. She was a beautiful woman, with a tiny waist and icy blond hair. Her blue eyes had fluttered at him with a coy flirtatiousness that left him cold. She wasn't *her*.

The Princess stepped out of her carriage and walked up the stairs to meet them. His parents greeted her and then she turned to him, expecting some show of gallantry. The wedding was to happen in less than a week. He forced himself to wear a mask of bland graciousness, but all he felt was despair.

He offered her his arm and led her into the castle.

A few hours later Prince Maximilian stood outside his pleasure slave's door. He had flatly refused to keep Jillian hidden for dinner. That was sure to set a bad precedent. He took a deep breath, realizing he was nervous. The guards opened the door and stepped aside, letting him see her for the first time all day.

She was glorious.

Her maids had outdone themselves this evening. Her hair was caught up in the topaz headpiece he had given her, the one that matched her eyes. She wore the matching earrings and bracelets as well. The bracelets reminded him of the cuffs he had made for her, the ones he could use to arrange her body for his pleasure. He felt his groin tighten. She aroused him by simply standing there.

He stepped forward and fitted the chain into her jeweled collar. He gripped the chain tightly. The weight of it felt reassuring in his hand.

She was his.

"Come, Jillian."

She lifted her eyes to his briefly and glided past him. She looked calm. He was relieved, fearing that she'd be angry at him... or ashamed. He knew it was cruel, forcing her to parade her half naked flesh in front of the Princess. It was so obvious that her beauty was displayed solely for his eyes. But it was the law that he could select a woman for his pleasure and he had done so. The sooner the Princess adjusted to the situation the better.

He watched his love slave's hips sway gently as he followed her through the castle. He would have her tonight, right after dinner he decided. Tonight and every night, marriage be damned. If he had to visit his bride once or twice a month to impregnate her, so be it. It would be Jillian he imagined beneath him. Perhaps with the lights off it wouldn't matter.

Tonight he would use the cuffs. He smiled, imagining her tied spread eagle on the bed. He'd tease her at first, and then-

"Good evening, Your Highness."

The Prince nodded to the courtiers as he followed Jillian into the dining room. She took her seat at the table with Sephina, his father's woman, and he joined his parents on the raised dais where they ate. A moment later his bride arrived. Everyone stood as Princess Letticia came into the room.

She looked particularly lovely tonight, her blond hair artfully arranged. Her figure was on display in a tight fitting icy pink gown. She certainly knew she was beautiful. She smiled at the Prince, expecting to be lavished with compliments. But his eyes were on Jillian. He couldn't help but want to gauge her reaction to the Princess's arrival.

His love slave was staring down at her plate. She looked outwardly composed but her face was white. He knew she hated this. She had been about to marry a Duke after all. She is the one who should be a bride, not this sniveling Princess he was being forced to wed.

He kissed the Princess's hand, noticing the malice in her eyes as she stared at his Sofriquette. It twisted her features, making her ugly. They sat down and were served wine. The Princess sipped hers quietly for a moment. He felt his eyes slipping to Jillian again. Sephina was speaking to her in a low voice. He wished he could hear what they were saying.

"Must we dine with your whore?"

The Princess's voice rang out over the room. Everyone froze, even the servants who were carrying platters of food. Maximillion found it difficult to breath for a moment. He closed his eyes, afraid to look at his sweet girl. He knew he would shatter if he saw pain on her face.

"She's not a whore."

It was his mother. His mother had leapt to Jillian's defense before he could react.

"We are very lucky to have Jillian and Sephina here. I suggest you never use that word again."

The Princess huffed a bit beside him but the Prince's eyes were on his Sofriquette. He saw the humiliation wash over her. None of this was her fault. He had done this to her. Put her in this untenable position. Because of his desire.

Sephina's hand was covering Jillians. He reminded himself to thank her. Thank God she was there. Jillian's beautiful head was held high, her chin raised slightly. He wondered what it cost her to sit there, unmoving.

He deliberately ignored Letticia for the rest of the meal, making no effort to conceal that his attention was elsewhere. She fumed beside him silently. The marriage was off to a miserable start but he didn't care. He didn't care about anything.

They were just serving desert when he stood abruptly. He'd had enough. He wanted to claim his woman and take her upstairs. He wanted to lose himself in her.

Jillian stood as the guards approached her. She looked bewildered at their early departure but she did as was expected. She walked slowly from the room. He knew she would want to know why they were leaving before the meal was finished. He debated about telling her. He certainly didn't have to answer to her or anyone.

His eyes roamed over her bare back as they walked through the caste to her chamber. As soon as they reached her door, he was pushing his way inside. He pulled her in behind him and slammed the door, pressing her up against it.

His mouth was on her in an instant. He kissed her deeply, feeling her reticence. He pulled back and looked down into her beautiful face. She was looking down and away, anywhere but at him.

"Look at me."

She seemed to brace herself before she lifted her eyes to him. They were awash with tears.

"It doesn't matter. None of it. Do you hear me?"

He held her chin, forcing her to keep her face raised. She shifted her eyes down, ashamed. Hot rage filled him. She wasn't going to melt into his arms tonight. He could tell. But she would do as she was told.

"Fine. Sulk if you want. But you will be of service to me. Take your clothes off."

Her startled eyes found his but he did not waver, looking at her coldly. She inhaled and stepped away, her hands going to her collar.

"Leave it."

She said nothing, her hands slipping to her dress where it was tied at her shoulders. She opened it and stood in her flimsy underthings, the firelight highlighting her perfect body. She was so lovely. And mutinous. She simply stood there, waiting. If she was going to make him spell it out, he would. He narrowed his eyes.

"The rest."

She stared ahead stonily as she peeled her camisole off her breasts and reached for her panties.

"Wait."

She froze, her hands on her lower stomach.

"Touch yourself for me."

She closed her eyes and slid her hands up to her breasts.

"Your nipples. Play with them."

She closed her eyes and made small circles on her nipples with her fingers. He knew she was aroused. They fed her aphrodisiacs at every meal. And she was primed from all the sex they'd been having. It didn't take much to make her ready for him. Still, he decided to delay things.

If she thought he treated her like a whore, he'd show her the difference.

Either way, he was going to have her. Again and again. It was going to be a long night. He smiled, feeling his cock swell in his pants.

"Help me undress."

She dropped her hands and walked to him, her hands going to his clothes and pulling them away efficiently. Coldly. He watched her dispassionately, hiding the emotions that were pinching his throat. She was trying to numb herself to him. But he wasn't going to let her do that. He grabbed her wrist and pulled her to the bed.

He lay down on the silk blankets, his nude body in the middle of the bed.

"You can take those off now."

She stood by the side of the bed uncertainly. He'd never done anything like this before. He knew she had no idea what he had in mind. He was being cruel he knew, but he couldn't stop. He wouldn't stop. She belonged to him no matter what and she would be reminded of that. *Now.*

She slid her panties down and waited. He looked her over, sliding his hand up and down his shaft. He was surprised at how aroused he was considering the mulish behavior of his bed slave.

"Come here Jillian."

She glanced at him, the nervousness in her eyes pulling at his heart strings. He squashed the feeling immediately. She would learn to be obedient regardless of the cost. She was crawling up the bed beside him but he stopped her.

"That's far enough. Take me in your mouth."

She froze and looked at his stiff prick, inches from her face. Then she lowered her head and pulled him into her mouth.

"Hmmmmm... yes, that's good. Work me with your tongue."

She complied, her tongue stroking his shaft as he resisted the urge to tousle her silky hair. He put his arms behind his head. He was going to distance himself from her if that's what she wanted. Every part of him except his cock.

He moaned as Jillian performed skilled fellatio on him, her lips gripping his shaft as her beautiful head moved up and down on his groin. She had really improved at this. Not that she required skill to arouse him. Her touch was enough.

"Enough. Take me inside you now."

Her eyes were adorably confused as she considered how to accomplish this. She moved above him uncertainly. He took pity on her and spelled it out.

"Straddle me."

He watched as she did as he asked, her tiny body stretched above him. He stared at her tight slit as she pressed it against the tip of his cock.

"Hmmm... yes... now hold yourself open so I can watch."

Her horrified eyes snapped to his. He stared into her eyes, making it clear that he meant what he said. Then he let his eyes drift down lazily over her lush body until he was staring at her cleft. Her fingers slid down and lifted her plump nether lips up and away. She was so small down there that it was only a small difference but the effect was incredibly erotic. She was totally exposed to him. He could see his shaft disappearing as she pressed her tight sheath down onto him.

"Hmmmmffff... good... now you may ride me."

He stared at her juncture, knowing it would disconcert her to be watched so blatantly. His hands were still behind his head as she started to move on him, her body undulating gracefully. He watched her sweet mound for a while longer before lifting his eyes to her face.

Her eyes were closed as she tried to hide her misery and her arousal as they battled within her. She hated being forced to perform for him. It was different when they made love but this was torturing her. He knew it but he didn't care.

"Open your eyes."

She whimpered for a moment before obeying him. She opened her beautiful eyes, staring out into space.

"Look at me. I want you to watch my face."

She whimpered and dragged her eyes to his face. He smiled at her coldly, then let his eyes wander back down to her slit, knowing she would see him looking at her there, owning her. She was breathing heavily now with pleasure despite her anger.

"Hmmm... you are close now, aren't you?"

She whispered something. He looked into her face again as she writhed on his cock.

"Answer me Jillian. *Are you close?*"

"Yes."

"I don't want you to finish yet. Take me in your mouth again."

She moaned as she slid off of him, kneeling between his legs. Her head lowered and rose on his cock. He was going to cum.

"Unfff... yes, hmmmm, I'm going to cum now Jillian. Pull harder... swallow..."

She sucked him harder into her mouth as his seed exploded from his shaft. She swallowed continuously as he filled her mouth again and again. He grunted as his cock jerked in her sweet, warm mouth.

Finally she lifted her head from his groin and sat back on her heels. She was fighting back tears... he could tell. But he did nothing to comfort her.

He stood up and crossed the room to the table. As usual there was a bottle of wine for her and a separate one for him. He poured himself a glass from her bottle.

"This is full of aphrodisiacs, isn't it Jillian?"

She nodded, watching him. He drank the entire glass and refilled it. He walked toward her, sipping her laced wine. Her eyes widened as she absorbed the implications. He held the glass to her lips, forcing her to drink.

"I assume it works on men as well. I want to be fully satisfied by morning. You are up to the task aren't you?"

He let his hand slide over her body possessively as he finished the wine. She whimpered in humiliation and arousal. He still hadn't let her cum. Maybe he would keep her on the brink until morning. Then he'd hold her in his arms while she cried and begged his forgiveness. Or he begged for hers.

He put the glass down and stood in front of her.

"Make me hard again."

He was already started to revive as she slid her mouth over his shaft, her tongue delicately swirling on the tip. She needed release desperately now and it made her perform with more passion than she'd shown earlier. He groaned as he watched her bottom in the mirror on the other side of the room. It gave him an idea.

"That's enough. Get on your hands and knees. Face the mirror."

She crawled backward onto the bed and turned, on all fours. The sight of her like that made his cock twitch eagerly. Her smooth haunches gleamed in the soft light as he moved behind her, pressing the tip of his shaft into her wet slit. He groaned as he slid in, resting his hands lightly on her hips.

"Look at me Jillian. I want to see your face."

She moaned and lifted her head, staring at him in the mirror. He let his guard slip as he slid in and out of her. His eyes stared into hers desperately. He wanted her to admit that he did not treat her as his whore. Not until tonight.

"Do you like being treated like a whore, Jillian?"

She was grunting softly as he pushed into her harder now, forcing the breath from her lungs in short bursts.

"Answer me! Do you like being used like a whore?"

"No."

He smiled slowly and reached underneath her to lightly stroke her clit.

"Are you *sure* you don't like it?"

"Oh, oh, oh, OH!"

He groaned as her sweetness convulsed around him. He pushed through her orgasm as she squeezed him, extending her pleasure and his.

"Hmmm... yes Jillian, that's a good girl...."

He stared at her as he pounded into her now, using her body for his pleasure. She came again as he felt his cock start to pulsate, his seed exploding into her waiting womb. He leaned over her body as they both shuddered their release. Then he got up and refilled his wine.

She started to rise, her movements unsteady.

"Don't move. I'll have you again in a few moments."

She froze, her head lowered as her shoulders trembled suspiciously. She was crying.

"You may lie on your stomach."

She did as he asked, laying face down, her head turned away from him. He stared at her and into the fire as he waited for his cock to rise again. It only took a few minutes, due to the aphrodisiac and the wicked thoughts he was having.

He moved behind her, covering her back with his body. He pressed his cock into her sweet hole, thrusting hard until he was fully seated. Her smooth round bottom felt incredible pressed into his stomach.

He pushed into her slow but hard, extending each stroke until he was nearly out of her body before driving back in again. He closed his eyes and let himself kiss her neck. He had been denying himself too. He let his hands stroke her buttery soft skin as his lips caressed her earlobe. Her soft sighs were like music to his ears. Perhaps they could reconcile now. Admit that they loved each other. He had told her once. But she had never told him.

He opened his eyes and looked at her in the mirror. Her face was turned to the side, trying to hide from him. She was grimacing in pain. He was hurting her. He'd used her too much, and too quickly. Again.

He froze.

"Am I hurting you Jillian?"

She whimpered, saying nothing. Her eyes were squeezed shut. He braced himself above her and pulled himself out.

"No matter. I'm tired of this little game anyway."

He stood and dressed, leaving her lying on the bed. He hated himself at that moment. But he was still so angry at her. She was all that mattered, why couldn't she see that?

"I suggest you improve your attitude tomorrow. If you need to be reminded of your position again, I am happy to do so."

He stared at her for a last moment. Then he strode to the door and left her. He paused after the door closed behind him, hearing her sobs. He had never left her like that before. He squared his shoulders and went to his room to brood.

The next morning he left her alone, not wanting to see the hurt look on her face. He already regretted his performance of the night before. He would be firm but gentle going forward. None of this was Jillian's fault. He didn't want her to be unhappy. He'd skipped lunch altogether, unwilling to sit through a meal staring at her.

He was walking with Letticia through the grounds, listening to her with one ear, when he noticed her guards were absent.

"I adore roses, don't you?

He looked around curiously, finally paying attention to their surroundings. They were in his mother's rose garden. Something was bothering him but he couldn't put his finger on it.

"Where are your guards?"

She smiled at him coyly, but there was something dark lingering in the back of her eyes.

"I gave them the afternoon off."

He frowned.

"I suspect they are entertaining themselves with your pretty little whore. I told them they could."

He felt his stomach drop out of his body as he turned on her.

"*You WHAT?*"

"I told them they could have their way with your whore."

He grabbed her shoulders roughly. She was smiling, her face full of spite.

"*WHERE ARE THEY?*"

"I have no idea. Honestly, who knew you would get so worked up over a little piece of trash."

She laughed as he ran off.

"I'm sure they are done with her by now!"

He was running through the gardens, his heart thudding in his chest. Oh god, if they'd hurt her... He ran faster than he'd ever run before. The castle was up ahead. He ran through the courtyard toward the barracks. His men were gathered in a group up ahead, looking at something on the ground.

He pushed them aside, staring at three of Leticia's guards. They knelt in the mud. They all looked as if they'd been in a tussle, each bearing several scratches on their faces. He stared down at them.

"Where is she?"

His voice was harsh and uneven. The kneeling men flinched. That's when he saw it.

Her hair. One of them was holding a swath of her beautiful hair.

"What did you do to her?"

"Nothing! She got away before we could-"

"Before you could what? Did you know she was the property of the crown? *My property!?!*"

The man nodded miserably.

"The Princess told us to mark her, to ruin her for you. She was jealous. I didn't want to hurt the girl-"

The Prince threw back his head and screamed.

"WHERE IS SHE?"

Behind her a feminine giggle met his ears. He turned to see Letticia standing with two of her ladies.

"Who knew a harlot could hold such power over a Prince?"

He turned his back on her.

"Please escort this bitch to the docks and put her on the first boat out of here."

"What? But you can't- the wedding is in two days!"

He turned back to her, a spiteful look on his face.

"I wouldn't marry you if you were the last woman on Earth. Now leave unless you want to end up like your men."

"My men? What about my men?"

He turned back to the terrified men.

"Did you touch her?"

The men looked at each other nervously. Finally they nodded.

"Where?"

"Just- her bosom and- to cut her hair- please show mercy-"

"Hold out your hands."

"No please, your highness."

"Shut up. *Hold out your hands.*"

The men held their hands forward. Max took a sword from one of his guards. He stared down at the men, their filthy hands. They'd touched her with those hands. One of them still held her hair. He reached down and pulled the silky strands from his grasp. That's when he noticed that there were small pieces of bloody skin attached. She must have struggled against them... He closed his eyes tightly.

When he opened his eyes again he wrapped her hair around his palm and grasped the sword. Without a word he lifted it and brought it down on the hand of the man in front of him. It sliced cleanly through his wrist, severing his right hand. The man screamed and fell back. Then he moved to the next man. He took one hand from each of them before dropping the sword.

"Make sure they live. I'm not through with them."

He turned to see Letticia leaning on one of her women, on the brink of a faint. She watched helplessly as her guards were dragged to the dungeons, screaming in agony.

"Be sure to tell your father it was an amicable decision to dissolve our betrothal agreement. Otherwise I will let word get out that you were bedding your guards."

Her eyes lifted to his, horror dawning.

"You can't! You wouldn't!"

"If you were a man, you'd be dead already. As it is, I'm sorely tempted to scalp you."

He turned and strode through the yard.

"JILLIAN!"

His guards trotted to keep up with him.

"Where is she?"

"She ran off- that way."

Another guard joined them from the other direction.

"She went into the smoke house. I saw her."

He started running. The smokehouse was at the far end of the castle settlement, bordering the woods. As it came into view his heart dropped.

The smokehouse was on fire.

He ran into the burning building, screaming her name. He could hardly see, but he reached out, feeling with his hands. His guards followed him in and pulled him backwards. It took four of them but they managed to drag him from the building moments before it collapsed.

"Noooo!"

The hoarse voice calling her name was not his own. The burned hands that clawed the earth were someone else's. The eyes that wept could not be his. He sat there and helplessly watched as the building burnt to the ground.

When the guards had finally managed to put the fire out, the Prince insisted on sifting through the rubble with them. No bones were found which gave him hope. But then, near the rear of the smoke house, they'd found the circlet of heavy gold.

Her collar.

The Prince said nothing. He ordered a search of the surrounding countryside but they all knew it was hopeless. She was gone. His love was gone.

Six months later Max was sitting at lunch with his father and Sephina. The Sobriquet had been visibly melancholy since the loss of Jillian. It seemed everyone was, even his mother. The Queen was out on a tour of the nation's religious houses, spreading wealth to the worthiest and making note of those that seemed to be languishing.

He ate sparingly. He knew they were all worried about him. He'd lost considerable weight since... the fire. He didn't like to think about what had happened but he couldn't stop himself. It was his penance for what he'd done to her.

He replayed their last night together over and over in his head, recalling the way he'd punished her. Remembering the look of humiliation and shame on her face as he'd forced her to perform for him. All he'd wanted was to sink into her arms and tell her he loved her, that he could never love the Princess. But his pride hadn't let him. He'd treated Jillian that way and then avoided her the next day until... He wondered if she had hated him when she died. He wondered if she'd felt pain.

Jillian.

Even her name caused physical pain to twist in his belly, like a knife. He knew that she had been hurt when Leticia's guards cut her beautiful hair. He knew that they had torn her dress off of her and touched her body. But they hadn't raped her. He was sure of it because he'd tortured them himself, making them retell their stories again and again. The men were still in the dungeon, brittle shells of human beings. He almost laughed. He was a shell too.

His parents were upset, not only because it seemed unlikely he'd be making an heir any time soon, but because he was disappearing before their eyes. The biggest chunk had gone the day of the fire. But little bits had been dissolving since, each time he thought about that last night, each time he listened to the men in the dungeon tell their tale... The only thing that helped was remembering the times he had made her happy. Or pretending that she was still alive... somewhere far from here.

A messenger ran into the room, bearing a small message with the royal seal. His father reached for it but the messenger bowed and held it to the Prince instead. He broke it open, his heart thudding in his chest.

His mother's handwriting. Three words.

I've found her.

Her? Did she mean-

He stood, his hands grabbing the messenger.

"Where?"

"The Hardcastle Nunnery. By the sea."

The Prince closed his eyes, afraid to believe. Then he ran from the room. It took a full day of hard travel with the Prince sleeping in his saddle. But by the next morning, he had arrived at the Nunnery.

The beautiful girl was sitting in a fenced courtyard playing with a lamb. The Prince was leaning against the perforated grate, staring at her as his mother tried to calm him.

"They found her in the woods. She was badly injured. She had fallen and struck her head on something."

He nodded, afraid to look away. It was her. Jillian.

She was alive.

"Max, she's not the same girl she was. She..."

"What?"

"She hasn't spoken since they found her. They've been calling her May. That's when they found her. She thinks that's her name. They think she might be... well, simple."

"It doesn't matter."

The Queen sighed and glanced at the girl through the fence. She was worried, he knew. Worried he'd just be hurt again. He didn't care though.

Jillian was alive.

"I'm going in now."

"Alright, son. Try not to be too disappointed if she doesn't remember you."

He kissed his mother and walked around the fence to the door in the gate. The Mother Superior stood there, wringing her hands.

"We had no idea who she was I swear to you, Your Highness."

"I know."

"You mustn't frighten her. She's terribly afraid of men. She's such a sweet child..."

He closed his eyes. That was his fault. He hadn't protected her. No one would hurt her again, not even him. He vowed it. He reached for the gate and stepped inside.

He took one step, two, three. The girl before him was laying in the grass on her side, her shoulder length hair gleaming in the sun. She had gotten a tan and filled out a bit. The nuns were apparently known for their cooking.

She looked beautiful.

As he got closer he noticed that she had scars now. A few around her shoulders where her hair curled against her jaw. Another on the swell of her breast where it pressed against the simple cotton dress she wore. They were scratches from when they'd tried to hurt her... but they hadn't.

He reminded himself again: she was safe. She was alive.

She looked up suddenly, staring at him wide eyed. He smiled at her, trying to be reassuring, trying not to frighten her with the intensity of his gaze. He longed to sweep her up into his arms. He wanted to touch her, to make sure she was real.

She was watching him warily, sitting up and clutching the lamb. The lamb started to bleat, trying to get away. In her fear she was squeezing it too tight.

He knelt down and sat in the grass a few feet away. He held his hand out to the lamb who escaped her grasp and trotted over to him. It sniffed his fingers and he scratched it's head, smiling shyly at the wide eyed girl.

She didn't recognize him. But she wasn't running away either. She watched him curiously as he played with the lamb. He looked up and her eyes were on his face. She was staring at his mouth. He smiled sensually and she looked away, blushing. At least he

195

knew the attraction was still there. On both of their sides.

He sat there in the grass with her until the bell tolled for the evening meal. He followed her slowly through the nunnery to the dining hall and took a seat across the room from her. He ate in silence, making an effort not to stare at her. He watched her surreptitiously as she ate, knowing immediately when she became aware of him.

She'd been reaching for more bread when she froze, staring at him. He acted as if it were normal for him to be there. Slowly, she would get used to him. The nuns were probably confused by the presence of a man in the room but they said nothing. He was the Prince after all.

They wouldn't allow him to sleep with or even near her, however. He was forced to sleep in the guest house reserved for men and married couples, located just outside the walls. His mother had returned to the castle and was sending back reinforcements. Guards. Lots of them. He wanted to make sure his love was well protected this time.

In the morning he wandered around, making sure he was always in her periphery. She did her chores, sweeping the walkways and taking care of the animals. He helped a few times. She looked happy. At peace. He knew he would soon shatter that peace by taking her back to the castle. But she belonged to him. There was no other option.

He was doing his best to be patient, once again sitting with her in the grass during prayer time. She was starting to be less nervous around him, even smiling at him when he fluttered his eyelashes at her flirtatiously. Her eyes were so soft now, with the innocence of a child. He wondered if she would ever regain her memories... he would love and protect her even if that day never came. His sweet girl was changed. He loved her anyway.

The lamb was joined with a bunny today, the animal seeming to follow her around. She was the one who saw to their feeding and they'd become attached to her. He was petting one of the silly lop eared rabbit when he heard her gasp. He looked up and her eyes were wide with fear, staring over his shoulder. In the gateway, he could see his guards. They must have just arrived.

Damn.

She was whimpering now, sliding backwards toward the stone wall. Her hand was cupping her temple where she'd injured her head. He'd noticed that she did that when she was afraid or unsure. He hated seeing her do that, wishing he could take her pain away.

If he hadn't noticed her holding her head, or known her before the accident, he would just thinks she was a beautiful simpleton. Sensual and sweet and naive. Perhaps he would even have selected her to be his Sofriquette...

He cursed and stood.

"Hush now, it's all right."

He strode to the gate and gestured his guards away. When he turned she was curled into a ball, weeping piteously. He scooped her up into his arms and walked through the nunnery. He found a nun who looked scandalized to see his Sofriquette cradled in his arms.

"Where is her room?"

She pointed down the hallway. He took off without a backward glance. Once inside her small spartan chamber he laid her down on her bed, then followed her down to the hard pallet, cradling her in his arms. She stiffened up and then relaxed after a moment, his hands sliding up and down her back comfortingly.

"I won't hurt you, my love. Shhhh... it's alright... everything will be alright..."

He looked down at her beautiful face to see her staring up at him. Her big eyes were full of wonder. She didn't remember him, not exactly, but she wasn't afraid of him. He had the strange feeling that she had taken a liking to him, on his own merits. Sh definitely liked looking at his face and his eyes. He felt warmth flood his insides at the thought.

"Jillian, I know you don't remember me, but I am here to take care of you. Alright?"

She nodded. He closed his eyes and pulled her closer.

"I promise, love. Do you remember the castle at all?"

She looked up at him, frowning. Her hand cupped her temple.

"Hush, it's alright. That's where you live. With me. We'll go back there soon and then you'll see."

She just stared at him. Eventually she fell asleep in his arms. The Nuns kept peeking in the room and trying to make him leave but he waved them off. He wasn't going anywhere.

In the morning he was there when she woke up. She watched him curiously as he washed up and pressed a kiss to her forehead.

"We are going home today, Jillian."

She just stared at him. He left to give the guards his instructions. They were to remain out of sight at all times. Several were sent ahead to arrange for every guard at the palace to swap their uniforms for casual clothes. They would still be there, but nothing would trigger her memory of the attack.

Once again he joined the nuns for breakfast, this time sitting beside her. After the meal the nuns gathered to say goodbye. Many of them were tearing up. She would be missed.

"Take care of her, Your Highness."

Jillian's eyes snapped to his face momentarily. Her hand lifted to her throat, as if she felt her collar again. He thought he saw a glimmer of recognition... then the dreamy blank look came over her face again. He lifted her to his horse and mounted behind her, pulling her back into his arms.

They rode slowly, barely above a walk. He wanted to enjoy the time alone and having her pressed into his arms. The ride would give them time to get reacquainted. And since his guards had rode ahead and cleared the roads and the woods, he could conceivably make love to her at any time. He was in a near constant state of arousal since they'd been reunited. Holding her exquisite body between his legs was driving him slowly insane.

The Prince forced himself to relax, hoping she would sense it and lean into his shoulder. It seemed to work. Her head was soon cradled in the crook of his shoulder. He let his hands move up and over her back. She wiggled a bit, clearly enjoying his touch. He held his breath and let his hands slide to her front, caressing the side of her breast.

She sighed deeply. He almost tasted his relief. She wasn't fearful of his touch. Slowly he moved his hand so that it circled over her nipple. She sighed again and arched her back, pressing her breast into his hand.

He chuckled, his fingers busying themselves with her nipples, playing with her breasts through her shirt. He was getting hard but she didn't seem to mind his arousal pressing against her bottom.

He held his breath and let his hand slip between her legs. He did nothing for a while, just let it sit there, pressing gently into her juncture. Her hips started to rock against his hand and he moaned, losing control. He lowered his head to hers, kissing her deeply. She responded to him warmly. She opened her mouth under the gentle pressure but did not press her tongue into his as she used to. Perhaps she had forgotten how to kiss...

His fingers swept down and pulled her dress up to the top of her thighs. Gently, he pulled one of her knee up toward the horses neck, spreading her thighs open. One hand held her thigh while his other snaked up to her cleft. He moaned into her neck, feeling her tight slit, now covered in soft curls.

He stroked her gently for a while, finally slipping a finger in between her plump little lips. Her head fell back as he worked his finger into her sweetness again and again. He played with her endlessly, finally bringing his other hand from around her narrow waist to her tender jewel. He alternated between circling her sweet little clit and toying with her breasts, keeping her aroused for an hour or more, always on the brink of climax.

He rejoiced in the soft sweet sounds of pleasure she was making. His engorged manhood felt like it would burst but he would not take her like a peasant by the road. This was about her, about prolonging her pleasure. In fact, he planned to spend the next week seeing that she was thoroughly satisfied as frequently as possible. No, the next *year.*

Finally he took pity on her frantic arousal. He pressed his face to her ear, whispering nonsense love words to her softly. All of his fingers were on her cleft now, one finger plunging in and out of her sweet well while another strummed her jewel rapidly. He felt her walls convulsing on his finger as her body arched in his arms. He murmured his encouragement as she shuddered, not stopping until he was sure she could not sustain her peak a moment longer.

He pulled her tighter against him as she trembled, tiny aftershocks of pleasure rolling through her body. She stared at him shyly, then rubbed her cheek into his shoulder. He chuckled and closed his eyes, willing his erection to dissipate. Slowly it settled down to half mast. It would have to do. He'd been chaste for so long. Too long.

They rode for another hour before the castle came into view. As ordered, the area was clear of guards. Of anyone really. The whole valley appeared to be deserted. It couldn't have been easy to do but as long as his precious girl wasn't frightened, he didn't care.

They rode into the bailey and he slid off his horse, pulling Jillian down into his arms. Then they walked through the castle. She barely looked around her. Perhaps it was familiar on some level after all. He escorted her to her chamber and took his leave as her maids cooed over her affectionately. They'd missed her as well.

She looked back at him and he closed the door. He was sorely tempted to stay and make love to her. But he was hoping the maids would help her remember. Not to mention that he needed a bath himself.

An hour later he was back to collect his Sofriquette for dinner. It was the first time they'd completed the ritual in almost seven months. He found himself nervous. He couldn't stop worrying about other people in the castle frightening her, or how she would react to him later in bed.

He knocked and opened the for to her chamber. Her maids kneeled immediately but she wasn't waiting with them. Jillian was staring into the mirror, tilting her head, her hand on the new collar they'd made for her. It wasn't jewel encrusted like the other ones she used to wear. There hadn't been time to make an ornate collar evidently. But they would remedy that tomorrow.

Her body looked beautiful in the soft silk amber colored gown she wore. But when she turned, he had trouble catching his breath. Somehow the changes in her over their separation had made her even more lovely. Her shorter hair curled around her face, making her kohl rimmed eyes seem even larger. The innocence in her gaze made her wide set eyes sparkle brilliantly. Her heart shaped face was sweeter than he remembered, set off by the subtle makeup and topaz jewels she wore.

He held his hand out and she walk forward, looking down shyly. He pulled out the gold chain and hesitated briefly before slipping the clasp onto the small circle in her collar. She was his. No one would doubt it after seeing them this way, least of all themselves.

She looked up at him, her mouth parting slightly. He stroked her cheek.

"Was there any trouble?"

"No, your highness. In fact, she went through the motions without any prompting."

He looked questioningly at her maid, Claire.

"Her body remembers."

He felt his groin tightening as he looked down into his pet's eyes. Her body remembered... they would see if that was true later tonight.

He sat eating with his parents, watching as Jillian was reunited with Sephina. He wondered briefly if anyone had thought to warn her about the changes in the younger Sofriquette. Sephina was nothing if not perceptive. He hoped she would help her... help her to heal.

Sephina looked at him briefly, a sad look in her eyes. It was hard to see Jillian this way, he knew. She was so bright and opinionated, even as his servant. He eyed the wine they were pressing on her. He decided to tell the powers that be that he wanted them to remove the contraceptive from it. The thought of his Sofriquette's belly swelling with his child suddenly made him feel very warm.

"How is she, son?"

His mother had taken a strong interest in the girl, particularly now that he'd refused to marry.

"It's too soon to tell but I think she remembers some things."

She nodded.

"Yes, that makes sense. I spoke to the doctor and he assured me that these things can take months or years to remedy. The brain heals slower than other parts o the body. And it can heal. Not always, and no entirely, but it can."

She laid her hand on his reassuringly. He smiled a her.

"Thank you, mother."

He looked back to the small table where the two women sat. Sephina's plate was empty but there was a small chocolate cake in front of Jillian. That was odd, they didn't often serve the Sofriquette's more than a small meal. He watched as the older woman encouraged Jillian to eat. She hesitantly picked up her fork and ate a bite. Then another. Slowly she made her way through the cake. She kept offering to share it but the older woman shook her head every time.

He sipped his wine, attempting to look away for a little while. He knew he was being obvious about where his attention was. Everyone in the room was probably aware of how much he anticipated the end of the meal. Finally he decided he had sufficiently diverted his attention. When he looked back, his mouth opened in surprise.

Something strange was happening to his love.

Jillian's eyes were closed and her body was rocking in the chair. Her head fell back and she lifted her hand to her collar.

They must have given her something. *Something strong.*

Sephina looked at him now, openly alarmed. He stood abruptly.

"Mother, father, please excuse me."

He felt himself rushing to her side. Jillian's eyes were closed as he looked at Sephina questioningly.

"They must have given her too much- or she' reacting differently since the accident. I don't know...'

She didn't have to say what they'd given her too muc of. He knew. *The aphrodisiac.*

He smiled at her tight lipped and pulled Jillian to he feet by her arm. Then he escorted her from the room Escorted was the wrong word. He *dragged* her.

He knew everyone was staring at them. Jillian always attracted stares with her beauty so provocatively displayed. But right now she was drugged, her body screaming out to be made love to. In her fragile state she had no pretense, no ability to conceal her reactions. Anyone who looked at her at this moment would know that she was primed for one thing: to be taken.

They practically ran through the castle to her chamber. Once inside he released her arm and stared at her, breathing heavily. She was also panting, her chest heaving as she stared at him. She was utterly confused by what was happening to her, he could tell. She grasped the collar around her neck and wrapped her other arm around her middle, moaning.

He crossed the room to her in an instant. She was staring up at him, confused by the feelings coursing through her body.

"Shhhhh... it's alright my love. I will take care of you."

He cursed, wondering why the chefs had done this. Obviously they wanted him to enjoy his reunion with his Sofriquette, but at what expense? He reached down and caressed her breasts, making her moan. He quickly removed her dress and picked her up, laying her nude body on the bed. Her maids hadn't bothered with underthings tonight. Apparently everyone had the same idea.

He stood and stripped quickly, his body hard, already responding to the sight of her beautiful body, writhing on the bed. She was rocking her hips and panting, craving a release she didn't know how to ask for.

He knelt at the foot of the bed, sliding his hands up her silky legs to her juncture. He lightly stroked her nether lips, once again bare for his pleasure. They both moaned as he slid a finger inside her. He lowered his head and pressed his lips to her jewel, flicking rapidly. There was no time for preamble. He wanted nothing more than to soothe her need.

He wondered if it would be enough. If the drug would wear off if he could bring her to climax. He didn't have long to wait.

His tongue lapped at her sweet petals now, his finger strumming against her nub. Her hips were flexing off the bed. She did nothing to hide her arousal. She was much more raw than ever before, nakedly hungry for his attentions. He gave them to her with all the skill he could muster, plunging his tongue in and out of her tight slit.

Then he felt her convulsing. Sweet sounds of pleasure greeted him as he continued his task, not stopping until he was sure she could not climax any longer. She was breathing heavily as he sat up, his hands on her thighs. He watched as she started to writhe again, the desire once again rising in her. She'd gotten less than a few moments of respite...

The Prince had planned to make love to her slowly, seeing to her pleasure again and again before taking his own. He saw now that it would be impossible. She didn't want his gentle teasing tonight. She needed to be taken. He wanted to take her. He growled and gave into his desire.

He held his throbbing member, edging it forward until it pressed against her slick nether lips. He braced himself on his forearms as he pushed inside her. She was nearly as tight as she'd been the first time, snuggly holding him in her tight sheath. She clenched around him, already starting to press her mound into him. He wasn't even fully embedded yet but the urge to plunge into her wildly was rising in him.

She whimpered and he realized that she wanted the same thing. This was a mating, pure and simple. He groaned and unleashed his lust, sliding home and then swiftly withdrawing, again and again. He pounded his stiff shaft into her willing body over and over, both of them crying out wordlessly as he brought her to another orgasm.

Her body shuddered beneath him and he lost control. His hips jerked as his seed filled her body, more than ever before. He'd been celibate the entire period of her absence, not even pleasuring himself as he'd used to. He'd only found release in dreams, like a green boy. And now she was the receptacle of all that pent up energy. He felt white hot pleasure as he released his essence into her endlessly.

He held her in his arms for the rest of the night, taking her twice more and stroking her to completion several times in between. Her restlessness continued till dawn. Tomorrow he would make sure they didn't drug her this way again. Tomorrow he'd tell them to stop the contraceptive. He lowered his head to her breasts, pulling a nipple into his mouth.

Tomorrow.

PART FIVE - MAXIMILLION

The Prince ran his hands over Jillian's soft skin.

She murmured in her sleep and he froze, hoping she would speak. It had been over two months since his pleasure slave had been returned to his keeping, and she had yet to utter even one word.

It was early morning. He had time to have her once more before the day began. As usual, he felt the need for her rising in him. He leaned down and whispered in her ear.

"Wake up, my Pet."

She rolled over and smiled up at him. He was coming to know her moods now, even without the benefit of speaking. She was a different person than she'd been before the accident, more innocent and with less of her stubborn pride. He kept hoping she would regain her old spirit, but he had to admit her lack of resistance to his desires was hard to complain about

Even without the aphrodisiacs, she did whatever he wanted without a moments thought.

"Open."

She slid her thighs apart, staring up at him adoringly. Her beautiful body was nude and her nipples thrust upward toward him, perpetually hard from the creams they applied to her skin. He'd insisted that she not be drugged with stimulants or contraceptives anymore, but the groomers had their own tricks. He hadn't bothered to stop those, especially since they were so delightful.

He lowered his lips to her luscious globes, licking and sucking her nipples into his mouth. His hand wandered to her inner thigh, making lazy circles on her tender flesh. He used the lightest of touches, making her squirm in her need. He'd had her twice already the night before, this time he intended to take his time.

"Jillian, can you say my name?"

She blinked at him, her need battling with her confused state. She'd lost her memory and ability to speak. He kept trying though, hoping he could bribe her into remembering with pleasure. The old Jillian would be annoyed with his teasing but now she just whimpered and rocked her hips, striving to bring her cleft closer to his fingers.

He smiled at her and kissed the frown marring her lovely forehead.

"Shhhhh, it's alright. It doesn't matter, love."

He took her mouth in a passionate kiss and let his finger slide up and down her nether lips. She was so wet already. She was the perfect concubine, the perfect mate. Her beautiful body responded to him so quickly and she was without any of the maidenly shyness she'd had before. He'd loved making her blush though.

He moaned as his finger slid into her sweet well. Her eyes closed and she started circling her hips as he pleasured her at his own pace. His finger moved in and out slowly, keeping her on the brink. Finally he withdrew and leaned over her.

Her eyes opened, imploring him without words to give her release. He couldn't tear his eyes from her as she thrashed desperately on the bed. With a groan, he sunk into her, his shaft stretching her tight opening wide. He eased in gradually as always, she was such a small girl, he never wanted to hurt her and he knew he was larger than most men. Not to mention being almost two feet taller than her.

Her wet warmth held him snugly as he started to move. His chest hair brushed her nipples with each long, slow thrust. She started making the sweet sounds she always made when she was close to climaxing. That, at least, was the same.

He held her in his arms as he picked up his pace, surprised at his own urgency. Would he ever get enough of her? It was doubtful, even if she never regained her memory or sharp wit. His hips flexed rapidly as he felt her body convulse around his manhood, pulling him deeper. He groaned as he felt his seed start to erupt from his cock head.

"Oh god! Unffff!"

His essence poured out of him and into his precious pet as she tossed her head wildly beneath him. He thrust into her again and again until he was spent. He rolled to the side, bringing her with him, still inside. He didn't want to leave her sheath an instant sooner than necessary.

Their bodies cooled as he let his hand slide up and down her back to her rounded bottom. He grasped her there, wondering if his seed would take hold this time. Or perhaps it already had.

Maximilian was preparing documents with his father when he heard the sound of his guards running. He stood and faced the door to the study as it slammed open.

"Your Highness!"

"Yes?"

"It's your Sofriquette. She cannot be calmed. We've called for the doctor but-"

He cursed and ran past them, shouting as he ran.

"Where?"

"The courtyard by the barracks."

That's where it had happened. Oh god.

The guards ran with him as they ran out of the castle and around toward the barracks. A small archway separated the two courtyards. That's where the soldiers from Haight had attacked her. Had tried to-

He pushed the thought aside as he saw her. His sweet Jillian was pressed against the wall with a dagger held out in front of her. She looked wild, with her hair in disarray and tears streaming down her face. She looked terrified- and angry. She looked aware.

She remembered.

"Jillian?"

"Max?"

She knew better than to call him that. But as children she had delighted in flaunting convention and often teased him with the nickname. Still, the sound of her voice was music to his ears.

"Shhhh- it's alright, Pet. Put the knife down. No one will hurt you."

"They- they had a blade. And they-"

"I know. But they aren't here. That was a long time ago."

"It was?"

"Yes. Please, Jillian. The knife."

She looked down at her hand as if surprised to see she held a weapon. She let it slip from her fingers to the ground. He ran forward and gathered her into his arms.

"Shhhhh, it's alright. Come inside with me."

He led her back inside the castle and back to her chamber. Her maids scurried to bring food and drink. He also sent for the doctor.

He sat in the chair by the fireplace and held her on his lap. She had her face pressed against his chest. He knew she was hiding from him.

"Jillian, do you remember what happened to you?"

She nodded, her face rubbing against his shoulder.

He smiled and continued to stroke her soothingly.

"Look at me."

She sighed and lifted her face begrudgingly. His smile widened, seeing her stubbornness returning before his eyes.

"No one will ever hurt you again. I promise you."

She looked down and away, biting her lip.

"Jillian."

He grabbed her chin and lifted it, staring into her eyes. There was something there. Shame.

"Do you believe me?"

"Yes, Your Highness."

"How do you feel? Does your head hurt?"

"No. Your Highness. I'm- I'm fine."

"Good. I've been beside myself worrying about you. For much longer than you know."

She looked away, being disobedient again. He'd have to get used to that side of her again. It was always stimulating to match wits with her. He grinned happily.

"I'm glad to have my spoiled little brat back."

Her eyes flared at him indignantly but she said nothing. She was smarter than that. She'd never flagrantly break the rules. He laughed.

"Go on, I know you are holding something back."

She shook her head 'no.' He squeezed her hips.

"Jillian. Do I as I say. Tell me."

She inhaled sharply. She hated being told what to do
Especially since she had no choice whatsoever.

"What is the matter?"

"I know time has passed. We've been continuing on a
before but to me-"

"Yes?"

"To me... It's yesterday."

He closed his eyes. Of course. The past few months and the six she'd spent in the nunnery must be a faint blur to her. In her mind, she'd just been attacked and he'd- oh god.

Her cheeks were burning as he stared down at her. He knew she was remembering the night he had punished her. He'd used her roughly and without care for her feelings or pride. He'd been trying to make a point of course. He hadn't meant it. But the next day...

"Jillian. I didn't mean what I said that night. I didn't mean any of it. I was angry."

She nodded, looking down and away.

"I've been spending every night making it up to you. I'll never use you like that again. Do you remember?"

She nodded again.

"Yes, but it's hazy. It feels like it's all been happening to someone else."

He pulled her into his chest again.

"We'll talk of this more sweeting. But for now I want you to rest. You can skip eating in the dining hall today. The doctor will be here soon and we'll hear what he has to say."

He unlocked her collar, setting it aside.

"What of-"

She stopped short, chewing her lip again. He sighed. It was really like playing a game of cat and mouse with her.

"What is it?"

"Nothing. It's not my place to ask."

He gripped her chin again.

"Jillian."

"I was just wondering what had become of your bride?"

He smiled grimly.

"She's gone. For good."

"Oh."

He could feel her wanting to ask him a million questions but she was right, it wasn't her place. She was there to serve him. The future queen was of little concern to her, even though the woman could make her life a living hell if she so chose to. Little did she know, he had decided not to marry for exactly that reason.

The door opened then and the doctor stepped in. There would be time to deal with all of this later.

The next week was spent nurturing Jillian's memory. He allowed some of her friends from before to visit her. The silly little debutants she used to surround herself with paled in comparison to his lush concubine as he watched them walk through the gardens. Her mother also came, though that visit left Jillian in a strange mood. At night he came to her and took her but it was different.

Something had changed.

The Prince could see that even though her body responded to his, she was not content. He told himself it would change in time. She'd been through so much. Surely he couldn't blame her for harboring resentment towards him for it. But he found himself resisting the urge to punish her for her reticence. He had to tease her body relentlessly into giving him the wild release he'd come to crave from her.

Finally he asked for her to be given aphrodisiacs again, starting tonight. He felt a little guilty about it, but he would get what he wanted from her. He was determined.

He came to collect his pet for dinner. She stood at the window, wearing a gown of shimmering crimson. As usual, it hung low on her back, leaving little to the imagination. He felt his loins tighten in appreciation for her beauty. She turned and he saw the stubborn tilt of her chin.

"Come."

She was obedient as always. She crossed the room to him, her head held high. He looked her over, unsmiling this time. Her beauty seemed to taunt him, as it had before he'd claimed her for himself. Finally he lifted the chain and attached it to her collar. He saw her watching as he wrapped the gold chain and leather strap around his hand.

She followed the guards through the castle, her back ramrod straight. He watched her with narrowed eyes.

Perhaps some sort of lesson was called for after all. If she only knew what he had gone through for her, what he had sacrificed. He couldn't give her that kind of power.

But he could take it away.

Tonight, he would chain her. He'd use the cuffs made to restrain her in any position for his pleasure. Tonight he'd make her admit her desire for him. She would tell him she loved him tonight. Tell him she cared.

PART SIX - JILLIAN

Jillian sat at the table with Sephina, slowly eating and drinking her sparse meal. The familiar taste of aphrodisiacs was back in her food. She frowned, wondering about the change. Sephina attempted to cajole her but Jillian's mood was bleak, as it had been since she woke from her amnesia.

This was her life. Forever.

She hated it.

It wasn't the Prince who she despised. She knew she cared for him, wanted him, maybe even more than that. He'd awoken her body to the pleasures of making love with him, and she craved his touch. But she wanted it to be her choice.

The thought of watching him marry another would be unbearable. She couldn't go through it again. Not that she had a choice.

She was so lost in her own inner turmoil that she missed the dark looks she was getting from the Prince. Sephina put her hand over hers.

"He's upset."

"What?"

"I am afraid that something is very wrong, my dear."

Just then the servers placed a small chocolate cake in front of Jillian. The last time they had given her this dessert, she'd been unable to control her raging desire for the Prince, unable to be satisfied all night long. It was laced, overfull of aphrodisiacs. Why had they given it to her again?

She shuddered and looked up at the Prince. He was rubbing his finger across his wineglass. Sephina was right. He looked angry.

"Oh dear."

"I can't- I-"

Jillian was whispering but the sound of desperation was clear in her voice. Sephina's hand came down on hers, squeezing her hard.

"You must."

Jillian closed her eyes and whimpered.

"You remember then?"

She nodded.

"I remember this cake and what it did to me. Oh god."

"Be strong. You know you have no choice."

Jillian nodded and opened her eyes. She reached for her fork and slowly began to eat the cake. Her cheeks burned with humiliation as she felt the effects take hold almost immediately. Warmth flooded her body, centering between her legs. She moaned, resisting the urge to grind herself into the chair. She'd barely scratched the surface of the cake.

She bowed her head, fighting for control. She wouldn't look at the Prince. She couldn't.

She did.

He was smiling sensually at her. His hooded eyes were traveling slowly over her body, down to her breasts and up again to her flushed face. He grinned, rubbing his lips with a long finger. A shock went through her.

"Jillian, do not test him please."

She lifted her fork at the older woman's urging. She forced bite after bite down her throat. The feelings of arousal intensified with each bite. She closed her eyes in agony, tears rolling down her face. She felt Sephina adjusting her chair, trying to block her from view. But nothing could stop the Prince from staring at her from his seat above, watching her torment.

She finished the cake and sat there, her head lowered. Only a few crumbs remained on the plate. The Prince stood abruptly and stood beside her. He tugged on her collar with the chain and she stood shakily. She followed the guards as they led them back to her chamber.

The moment they were inside her knees buckled. He caught her against him and she felt his arousal press against her hip. He carried her across the room and lowered her to the chair.

"The cuffs."

Her maids scrambled to get the box containing the cuffs and chains. They quickly slid the cuffs onto her wrists and ankles, locking them firmly into place.

"Leave us."

He watched her from where he leaned casually against the mantle. She stared at the ground, crossing her arms over her chest. She was utterly defeated.

"Stand up."

Woodenly, she did as he asked. She felt him come closer, shivering as he ran his fingertips over her dress. Slowly, he slid it off her shoulders so that it pooled at her feet. She stood before him, her naked body glowing in the firelight.

He leaned down and kissed her. She whimpered as his lips pressed into hers. He forced her mouth open and plundered her with his tongue. She didn't respond quickly enough. He pulled back, an angry look on his face.

"Get on the bed."

She hurried to the bed and looked back to him, desperate not to anger him further.

"Spread your legs and lift your arms over your head."

She closed her eyes tightly, doing as he asked. She wanted to beg him not to torment her- to make love to her normally- but she knew he wouldn't listen.

And she could not say no anyway. She had no rights at all. She was his slave.

She heard him moving around the bed, heard the chains as they clinked against each other. He tied her wrists above her first, and then her ankles to either side of the bed. She felt so exposed...

"Open your eyes."

She forced herself to look up at the ceiling.

"Look at me, Jillian."

He stood by the side of the bed, fully clothed. He had a hard look on his face.

"Do you want me, Jillian?"

She moaned, nodding her head.

"Yes... please..."

He smiled coldly.

"Good."

He climbed onto the bed, his broad shoulders leaning over her. He started to run his fingers up and down her body, over her breasts and hip bones, down her legs nearly to her feet. Then up again, over and over until she was struggling against the chains.

"Do you want me to touch you here?"

He circled her nipple with his finger, not touching it.

"Ye- yes- oh god!"

He smiled and leaned down, pulling her nipple into his mouth. Her back arched as pleasure coursed through her body. He lifted his head, making her moan. He slid his hand down to her apex.

"Do you want me to touch you here?"

She was breathing heavily, hating him for doing this to her. She turned away from him, fighting back tears.

"Jillian! Look at me!"

She turned her head back, lifting her blazing eyes to his. He was staring at her with longing. He needed to hear it, she realized. She closed her eyes again. His finger drifted closer and closer to her center.

"Yes. I want you to- oh!"

He was between her legs suddenly, pushing himself inside her. He'd freed his cock from his pants without removing them.

"Unffff, oh god Jillian, I can't wait."

He pushed himself into her body and withdrew almost completely. Her flesh quivered around the tip of his shaft.

"Jillian. Tell me."

He was tenderly stroking the side of her face. She opened her eyes and stared up at him. She knew he was asking her for something she had never given him, or anyone else. She couldn't fight it anymore.

"I want you."

"What else?"

He kept himself just outside her body, tormenting her with need. But it was the look on his face that undid her resistance once and for all. He loved her. And she loved him. So for the first time, she said the words aloud.

"I love you."

He moaned and buried himself inside her, bucking wildly in and out. She found her release almost immediately, her hips flailing beneath him. He held her steady as he pounded into her flesh.

"Oh god, I love you Jillian. Oh god, yes!"

He threw his head back as hot sticky fluid pulsed into her. Her body responded, clamping down on him, sending her into another orgasm.

Finally he collapsed on top of her. He started kissing her face, tiny little kisses.

"I love you Jillian. I love you. Don't fight me anymore, please..."

"I won't. I promise..."

He leaned up so he could look at her.

"Did you mean it, Jillian?"

She nodded shyly.

"Yes. I love you, Your Highness. I do."

He moaned and wrapped himself around her. She whispered into his ear.

"If you untie me, I'll show you."

In the morning Jillian woke up to the Prince kissing her face. He was quickly making tender love to her yet again. She knew he loved her. It was obvious from the way he was touching her, the way he always touched her.

She had mixed feelings about admitting her love for him. It was just another way that he held power over her. He owned her completely now, even her heart.

She cried out in pleasure as he poured himself into her again. He seemed to take even greater pleasure in finishing this way now, rarely ever having her take him in her mouth. She wondered why but knew she wasn't supposed to ask. She could ponder the reasons though... Her mind at least, was still her own.

He left her afterwards, telling her he loved her again. She smiled at the memory. At least she wasn't alone in this love. And when he married, she would have his love if not his name or his child.

At breakfast she had a hard time eating her food. It was the one hearty meal of the day. Sephina looked on sympathetically as Jillian clamped her hand over her mouth.

"I'm going to throw up."

Sephina's eyes were wide as Jillian started to stand. Everyone stared as the Sophriquette broke all tradition and started to run from the room. Her chair brought her up abruptly, jerking her backwards. The Prince released it immediately, running to her side in an instant.

"Jillian! Are you alright?"

She threw up on the floor in the middle of the dining room. Chaos broke out as the Prince lifted her into his arms and carried her from the room. She looked up at him, mortified.

He was smiling.

An hour later she understood the reason. The doctor was speaking to the Prince in low voices just outside the door but she clearly heard the word "bed rest."

When the Prince came back inside, his green eyes were glowing with pleasure. She narrowed hers at him and started to rise from the bed. He was across the room and pressing her back down before she knew what was happening.

"You need to rest."

She stared at him mutinously, crossing her arms over her chest. He laughed.

He was so smug, it made her want to scream. She turned her head away, suddenly feeling tearful again. What was wrong with her?

"Oh Jillian, don't cry my pet."

He pulled her into his arms.

"I'm so happy. You're going to give me a child."

Her eyes widened and she bolted upright.

"What?"

He laughed again. He was always laughing at her. I he wasn't the Prince she would have smacked him.

"You're pregnant my love. That's why you threw up."

She paled and turned away from him.

It couldn't be.

"But I thought they took precautions for things like that- in my food..."

"I told them to stop a long time ago. After you disappeared. I want to have a child with you."

She choked back an angry retort. Her body curled in on itself as she started to weep in earnest. She tried to stop, to remember her position, but she could not.

"What is it Jillian? Aren't you happy?"

She only cried harder

.

"Answer me Jillian! That's an order!"

His voice rang out like a whip as he pushed her onto her back, forcing her to face him.

"Jillian!"

"No! I am not happy!"

The shock and hurt on his face struck her to the core
But she couldn't lie. Not about this.

"But- why?"

"How could I be happy to be bringing a bastard into
this world? Knowing you will marry and another
woman will bear your true heir? I'm sorry. I can't be
glad about doing that to a child!"

He stood and walked across the room. He leant on the
mantel, facing away from her. She braced herself. She
knew that her life was forfeit if she displeased him.

"Kill me if you must but please don't punish my
family for my honesty. You owe me that much."

251

He turned back to her, his eyes narrowed in disbelief.

"Kill you? Are you insane?"

She stood up, feeling unsteady on her feet.

"I disobeyed you. I know what the punishment is. I should not have mentioned your marriage."

He crossed the room and grabbed her tightly, slamming her into his chest.

"You stupid woman. I won't be marrying for political reasons. I'll be marrying for love."

"I don't care what you do to me. Just please, if you care for me at all, you won't make me force a child to watch their mother be your whore."

He grabbed her shoulders, spinning her. Sh
screamed, fearing the worst.

"Be still! I'm just trying to take your collar off."

She held perfectly still while he unlatched the heav
collar from around her neck. She stood while h
traced the faint impression of the collar in her skin.

"We'll get you a new one. A smaller one."

She spun to face him, outraged. He would choke he
That was to be her punishment!

He was laughing. He leaned in and kissed her.

"But this one will be for your finger."

Her eyes opened very wide.

"Will you marry me Jillian?"

She opened her mouth and closed it again, like a fish.

"Say yes, Jillian."

"Yes. Oh, yes!"

PART SEVEN - MAXIMILLION

The Prince smiled, going through the arduous grooming procedure required for formal events without a word of complaint. Usually he squirmed and sighed during the endless shaving and polishing but today he was preoccupied.

Today he would be married.

He grinned at his reflection. He knew he had done the right thing by releasing Jillian from her position as his pleasure slave. Her happiness alone had made it worth it.

He would miss seeing her in those outfits though... perhaps she'd wear them for him in private now and then. He wouldn't command her to do so though, he would ask.

Jillian had put him through his paces after agreeing to wed him. She'd grilled him with questions, the main one being centered upon her free will. Yes, she could refuse him and question him now.

She had bit her lip adorably. He had decided not to mention that as her husband he did have *certain* rights. He sighed. All that mattered was that she was happy.

It was time before he knew it. He walked through the castle to the Chapel, where his parents and half the nobles in the country were waiting.

He stood at the front of the church with the Priest and waited. The minutes ticked by and he started to get nervous.

Where was she? Had she changed her mind? Perhaps he shouldn't have given her her freedom in advance. Perhaps-

The doors opened as the music began. Before him, in a dress of silver and white, was his bride.

Jillian.

She was resplendent in her gown. Her beautiful hair was caught up in ornate twists under her heavy diamond crown. Her neck sparkled with a necklace.

It was the first time in months he'd seen her without her collar. It was the first time he'd seen her at all in *weeks*.

His mother had insisted on the separation for propriety's sake. Now that Jillian was a free woman, her rank and reputation must be considered. He had happily agreed, knowing he was getting what he ultimately wanted, sure he wouldn't mind the wait.

He had minded, of course. A lot.

He'd spent the past two weeks craning his neck and skulking around, hoping to see her. He'd been far too distracted to handle matters of state. Now he inhaled deeply, knowing it had been worth the separation.

She shone like the sun, her beauty overwhelming him. But it was the look of love in her eyes that nearly brought him to his knees.

She was here because she wanted him. Not because she had to be there. He'd given her the choice, risking everything. But he'd had to. He couldn't hurt her for one moment longer. She deserved to be free.

He smiled at the stunning creature walking towards him and held out his hand.

JILLIAN

Jillian sat on the edge of the Prince's bed in her silk underthings. No, now it was *their* bed. Her

258

possessions had been moved out of the Sophriquette's chamber above. The Prince had sent her a message about the move, asking that she forgo having her own chambers as was tradition.

She had decided immediately that his request was reasonable. But she had waited three hours to respond. She smiled, knowing that had driven him mad.

Perhaps that had been a little cruel...

The door opened and he stepped inside. He looked glorious in his formal garb. She smiled at him and stood, crossing the room to him.

MAXIMILLION

He stared down at her hungrily as his bride slid her hands up his chest, pushing his jacket aside. He barely spoke as she undressed him, both of them reveling in the knowledge that they were formally tied to each other.

He wanted her so badly. It was all he could do to hold back. But knowing that she was here of her own will, that she wanted him too… it was worth it.

Judging from the warm look in her golden eyes, she wanted him *now.*

"Get on the bed."

His eyes snapped open. Was she commanding him?

He grinned down at her. His bride wore a haughty, imperious expression. She *was* commanding him. He decided to play along.

"Yes Princess."

She forced a stern look on her face, following him over to the bed.

"You will give me pleasure tonight."

He fluttered his eyelashes at her, laying nude on the center of the bed.

"As you wish, Your Highness. What would you like me to do first?"

She frowned and chewed her lip, unsure of what move to make next in their little game. He growled and pounced on her, pulling her carefully onto the bed.

"Oh!"

He grinned down at her, caressing her body. His hand lingered over the soft swell of her belly. It was just beginning to round.

"I will serve you well your Highness. For many years to come."

He lowered his head to hers and took her mouth in a long, drugging kiss. Her back arched, pressing her body into his. He pulled back and teasingly pulled her silk slip up her body, casting it aside.

He grinned at her wolfishly as he caught her wrists, holding them high over her head. Her eyes widened, realizing the tables had been turned.

"Starting right now."

EPILOGUE

MAXIMILLION

He stared appreciatively at the woman standing before him. She was in front of the mirror, looking at herself in the sheer gold silk gown.

It laced up her back, revealing more than it concealed.

She smiled seductively at him, her beauty reflected in the mirror's surface.

Tonight, they were celebrating one year of marriage.

Tonight, she had donned the garb of the Sophriquette once again.

"Come, I have need of you."

She bowed her head slightly. Her steps were soft as she padded to the bed in her bare feet. He watched her, deciding to use the chains tonight.

He opened the box, watching her eyes grow large. She said nothing as he secured her limbs, pressing a kiss to each one in turn as he chained her.

A soft gurgle came from across the room. He held a finger to his lips as Jillian strained against her bonds.

"Be still, pleasure slave."

"But-"

"Shhhh... he's fine. Besides, this is the only way for me to have you to myself for a few hours."

She blinked up at him. She was a devoted mother. But right now, *he* was the one who required her devotion.

"Should I call the nursemaid?"

"You would not!"

He grinned.

"They've seen you chained to the bed before. Surely you remember my birthday?"

How could either of them forget? She'd been pregnant still, and he'd bargained for the privilege of keeping her on edge for hours. When she'd finally found release, her scream had brought half the castle running.

Maximillion had merely looked up from where his face was pressed between her thighs and told them to close the door behind them.

Then he'd made her scream in pleasure again.

He smiled, deciding that he'd have to muffle his Princess's screams tonight. After all, they did not want to disturb the future heir of the Kingdom with their vigorous lovemaking.

He pulled his tunic free and began.

THE END

COMING SOON FROM CALYOPE ADAMS

THE PRINCE'S POSSESSSION

"The Prince is back."

Lilly paused, her fingers deep in the soft dough. She stood a bit taller, knowing he would soon appear. She didn't know why she should care, even though he paid her too much attention.

Prince Damon never had anything good to say to her.

Ever since they were children, Damon had found reasons to criticize her. Her work, her dress, the way she wore her hair.

If he knew about her secret, hidden in her room, she had no doubt he would see her punished for it. But no one knew. No one save Old Bessie who had given her the book.

Slaves were not supposed to read.

Besides, she was punished often enough. As much as she loathed it, she had survived worse. She sprinkled more flour into the bowl and pressed harder.

"Day dreaming again?"

She jumped, her back stiff. The low, husky voice was inches away. His breath tickled the fine hairs at her nape.

Damon.

Or rather, Prince Damon, his royal highness.

She had no right to use the familiar name, the one she had learned before she could say more than a few words. The Prince had enjoyed playing with the castle children, several of which were slaves.

But right now, she was one of only two who worked in the kitchen. The rest were lowborn, but free.

A fact they enjoyed pointing out to her as often as possible.

A fact she loathed.

She held perfectly still as he reached past her to grab an apple from the high work table she stood at. He took a bite as he walked away, throwing her a smirk.

The look on his handsome face was so smug! She grit her teeth, kneading the dough harder. He made her heart race, yes, but it was because of his arrogance!

Of course, he was the heir to the throne of their small but wealthy kingdom, and she was less than nothing. A slave. A piece of property.

"Lilly! Pay attention!"

She scowled and lifted the dough from the bowl. It was ready to be rolled and then cut into smaller shaped for flat bread. It was servants food, but the King always included it in his meals.

Of course he dipped his in the finest of olive oils, seasoned with fresh herbs and salt.

Lilly sighed. She adored fine foods, often sneaking a taste after everyone else had eaten. Even the servants ate better, leaving only gruel and the rare stolen bite for Lilly or Old Bessie, the two kitchen slaves.

Not that Bessie did much work anymore. But she was kept on, as there was nothing else to do with her. She sat in the corner on a rickety chair, slowly peeling potatoes for the castle's evening meal.

Lilly reminded herself to bring the old woman a sip of water the next time she was allowed a break. She worked swiftly, willing the hours to pass.

"Son."

Damon smiled, still eating his apple.

"Father."

"How was your journey?"

He shrugged, sitting across from his father on a soft sofa in the sitting room. His father favored this room, with it's rich velvets and enormous hearth.

Of course all the rooms had fine furniture and were well heated, but this one reminded them both of his mother, the late Queen.

"Uneventful."

He was journeying through out the Kingdom, as part of his education. He'd had the finest tutors but it was the every day lives of the common man, as well as the lesser nobility he had to understand to be a good ruler one day.

"It's nearly your birthday son."

Damon nodded, eating his apple bite by bite.

"It's time for you to chose your concubine. I'm sure you haven't forgotten."

"I have not. In fact, I've already chosen."

"Have you? Someone worthy I hope?"

Damon smiled.

"Oh I'm sure she'll perform admirably."

"Who is it?"

He smiled and took the last bite of his apple.

"I've chosen Lilly."

His father exhaled, clearly exasperated.

"I suppose I'm not surprised. You've always had an unhealthy fascination with the girl."

Damon smiled wolfishly.

"I'd say it's entirely natural."

"I admit she's uncommonly lovely." He shook his head. "Well, if you are certain you won't grow bored with an untrained-"

"I'm certain. I've never owned a slave. I think it's time."

"You know I've been trying to ease the country away from the practice. We don't breed them anymore."

"I know. But I want her. I want to own her."

"It's a big responsibility. You must be prepared to punish her if she'd disobedient. She's always been willful."

"I know. I look forward to it."

"It's your birthday, Damon, and your choice. But you only get to choose once…"

Damon smiled.

"It's what I want."

"She'll be examined and presented to you at your party."

"Thank you father." He stood and bowed. "My King."

EXCERPT OF TAKEN BY THE VIKING

RANULF

Ranulf followed the other warriors through the burning wooden door of the Saxon Nunnery. It was the only entrance through the high stone walls that surrounded the enclave. They'd set fire to the ten foot doors a few hours ago and then broken through the weakened wood with their axes. In the interim, they'd already gathered up the livestock and anything else worth taking from the surrounding farm land. But it was the wealthy religious house that was their true target.

Now they were in, and the pillaging would begin in earnest. Ranulf looked around, his blue eyes scanning the room for valuables. He stood head and shoulders above the other, already enormous Vikings, so he had a clear view of the carnage as it unfolded.

He grimaced as one of the Vikings threw a young Nun over his shoulder and looked for a place to run with her. He didn't agree with harming innocents in such a way, though he was one of the few. Willing women were too plentiful for him to ever feel the need to take a woman by force.

Especially not a Nun.

"Ranulf! You gather and sort the women!"

There were wails filling the air as the women gathered in the chapel, thinking that the sanctity of the place would save them. Of course, the Norsemen had their own Gods, and none of them gave a pip for their sanctuary. He waved the remaining women into the room.

"Come on now, in here. Let's get you sorted."

He was the one who was usually given the task of sorting the women. Not only did he speak the Saxon tongue but he had the best eye and a soothing way with the fair sex. His good looks were certainly a part of it.

Although he was among the largest of all the men, his body was fit and lean under his massive shoulders. He had twinkling blue eyes, a handsome craggy face with high cheekbones and a square jaw. His nose was straight and not over large. Remarkably, it hadn't yet been broken, something the men teased him about mercilessly.

His smile was winning as he peeled back his well formed lips to reveal white straight teeth. With his light blond hair cast back over his shoulders, he looked a bit like an angel to the sisters. They stared up at him with less trepidation than one might expect under the circumstances.

"Alright, we'll be making three groups of you. No need to struggle or fight. If you run, one of them will catch you and between you and I, they are pretty worked up at the moment. Better to avoid aggravating them."

The women quieted and watched as he walked through them. He tapped some to be kept (strong looking), others to be sold (comely), and the elderly and infirm to be left behind to fend for themselves.

He worked his way through the room, the women standing more or less agreeably in their new groups.

The crowd parted and he found himself staring down at a stunning young woman. Huge green eyes stared up at him from a face of indescribable beauty. Her smooth skin was glowing, her high graceful cheeks rosy, and her plump red lips the sort that begged for a man's kisses. Her long dark hair was unveiled, and her shapely body was revealed by the thin nightclothes she wore.

"Ranulf?"

His jaw dropped. A flash of memory came over him. He stared in awe at the suddenly familiar face. Could it be her?

"Kayla?"

"Aye! You remembered me!"

"Of course I do. What are ye doing here?"

"My father sent me away after I refused to marry."

"Why on earth would you do that, girl? You knew he had a foul temper."

"I had already promised myself to someone."

He felt himself growing annoyed with this mysterious personage. He frowned sternly.

"And who might that be?"

"You! Don't you remember, Ranulf?"

He frowned, worried that her father had hurt her on his behalf. And for no reason! They had not wed, nor spoke again since that long ago summer as children.

"We were just wee children then Kayla. It was a silly game. You should not have risked so much."

"Well, I know that now, but at the time I was only seven!"

"You've been here this whole time, then?"

"Aye. My father did not take kindly to my promising myself to a Viking."

She smiled up at him wryly as he resisted the urge to gather her up in a bear hug. It had been so long since he had seen her. They both lived on either side of the border between their lands and both had a natural tendency to explore. They had met unexpectedly on the sea shore as children and formed an unlikely bond.

He was still staring, dumbstruck at his incredibly lovely childhood friend as the smile faded from her face. She leaned in conspiratorially, speaking in an urgent whisper. The Nuns around them were transfixed, hanging on their every word.

"Ranulf, do you know what they are going to do with us?"

His stomach dropped. He did know indeed. Her exceptional beauty would make her a target for all the men. They'd fight over her, possibly hurting her in the process. She'd be used up well before she got to market to be sold, her virtue stolen and her beauty bruised and marred. After that she'd be sold to a brothel most likely.

A sick feeling settled in the pit of his stomach at the thought. He could not allow that to happen. He *would not.*

Loud shouting came from outside the chapel, causing the women to back away from the door. His head snapped up and he shook himself.

What was he thinking, having a nice chat with a pretty girl in the middle of a raid? If he was going to do something, he had better do it. Right now. He looked down at Kayla and tried to convey the urgency of his instructions.

"Nothing's going to happen to you. I'll make sure of it. But you must do exactly as I say. Don't struggle."

"What?"

"Hush now, woman."

Ranulf took a cloth from his pack and stuffed it in her surprised mouth, quickly tying a rope around her head, gagging her effectively. He grabbed a cloak off of one of the other Nuns and wrapped it around Kayla, covering her hair. Her eyes were wide as he tied her hands and tossed her over his shoulder.

"Fare ye well, ladies. Remember, stay calm and docile and it will go better for ye all."

He left the chapel, kicking the door shut behind him with his boot.

"Have you finished then, Ranulf?"

"Nearly. I decided to take my share now. You can finish up can't you Ulfrik?"

The older man nodded and Ranulf clasped his shoulder. He was a good choice. He wouldn't frighten the women over much. If they started to panic anarchy would break out and that was the last thing he needed. It was best to keep a low profile when stealing a treasure for oneself, especially one so precious. He strode through the stone halls to the front gate where his horse waited.

"What have ye got there Ranulf?"

Ranulf slapped his hand over Kayla's rump, making her squeal into her gag.

"I've decided to take my share now."

"A woman? That's unlike you Ranulf. You always want gold or supplies for your new home."

"It's time I had a nice thrall to warm my bed. I took a liking to this one."

"Let's have a look at her then."

"Erm, not right now Sturla. They need your help with carrying the mead."

Sturla's eyes lit up. He was overly fond of drink. He eyed the horses nervously.

"Are ye sure Ranulf? I'm supposed to watch the horses."

"I can do it for ye! I've already taken what I want. Go ahead then."

Sturla didn't have to be told twice. As one of the lowest ranking warriors he got the worst assignments. His share of the haul was usually slim pickings, if anything was left over at the end of a raid.

Ranulf strode to his stallion, Guda, and carefully laid Kayla over top of it, doing his best not to jostle her overmuch. He busied himself with his horse, pretending to be repacking his kit so no one would ask why he was out here instead of inside, where the action was. Kayla tried to lift her head, sending her dark silky hair tumbling out of the hood. He reached up and gently tried to stuff it down her back.

"Be still Kayla, I won't harm ye. I had to think of something to get you out of there, ye understand?"

She made a series of noises. He had no idea what she was saying but she sounded at least somewhat agreeable. He patted her shoulder awkwardly.

"There, there. I'll get you out of here and safe and sound in my hut. Then we can see about getting you home."

He'd given up his share of the raid but it was well worth it to save his friend. Besides, he'd gotten a goblet or two from the chapel, now stashed securely in his satchel. They all shared the profits from the sale of any of the slaves as well.

He unrolled and rolled his bed pack several times, unwilling to leave her side. It wasn't likely that anyone would bother with something strapped to his horse, like the bundled up woman, but he couldn't leave it to risk. They were Vikings after all.

"Would you look at that! Ranulf's got himself a woman!"

Halldor and Valgard were approaching, large satchels of stolen goods over their shoulders. The raid must be nearly over, Ranulf realized as men poured from the gate. A quick and easy one then. The bear like Halldor was laughing but Valgard looked suspiciously at the bundle on Ranulf's horse.

"Best not be. My sister's had her sights on him for herself."

Ranulf ignored Valgar. His sister Astrid was a blowzy blond, large breasted and big mouthed. Sure, many men would like to tumble with her, but she wasn't to Ranulf's liking. He preferred small dark haired women. Women more like Kayla, though he'd never seen one near as lovely. He wondered briefly if that's where the preference had started.

"Well, he can always have two!"

Halldor laughed and slapped the surly Valgar's shoulder. The men unloaded their goods and started climbing onto the horses. A steady stream of women tied together around the wrists and waists, followed them into the road. They were off.

Ranulf pulled himself onto Guda and lifted Kayla up so that she was sitting upright in front of him. He slowed their pace so he was out of the thick of the pack.

"Keep your hood down and your face hidden. I don't want anyone to get a good look at you."

She murmured into her gag again. He allowed himself to relax a bit. They were nearly home free. He grinned, enjoying the feel of her feminine body in his arms.

"Are ye thirsty?"

She nodded, peeking up at him from under her hood.

"I'll take the gag out but just for a moment. No talking right now, ye hear?"

She nodded again and he pulled the gag down and lifted his wineskin to her lips. She drank greedily, a trickle of red escaping her lips. He wiped the wine from her chin and tucked the gag back into place.

"Alright?"

She nodded and he pulled her close, angling her face away from the other men. He settled a stony expression on his face and laid his hands possessively on her hips and thighs as if he were just another Viking taking home a woman to bed. That should allay any suspicions the men might have at his sudden interest in unwilling females.

ABOUT THE AUTHOR

Calyope Adams is an author of historical erotic romance.

ALSO BY CALYOPE ADAMS

Taken By The Viking

.

Made in the USA
Lexington, KY
24 June 2017